Cookie Chronicles BOOK ONE

BEN YOKOYAMA

AND THE COOKIE OF

DOOM

THE COOKIE CHRONICLES

Cookie Chronicles BOOK ONE

BEN YOKOYAMA AND THE COOKIE OF DOOM

BY MATTHEW SWANSON
& ROBBI BEHR

A YEARLING BOOK

Text copyright © 2021 by Matthew Swanson
Cover art and interior illustrations copyright © 2021 by Robbi Behr

Visit us on the Web! rhcbooks.com

Educators and librarians, for a variety of teaching tools, visit us at RHTeachersLibrarians.com

The Library of Congress has cataloged the hardcover edition of this work as follows:
Names: Swanson, Matthew, author. | Behr, Robbi, illustrator.
Title: Ben Yokoyama and the cookie of doom / by Matthew Swanson and Robbi Behr.
Other titles: Cookie of doom
Description: First edition. | New York: Alfred A. Knopf, 2021. | Series:
Cookie chronicles; 1 | Audience: Ages 8–12. | Audience: Grades 4–6. |
Summary: Eight-year-old Ben takes a fortune cookie literally, and believing he has only
one day left to live, tries to do everything he has always wanted to before nightfall.
Identifiers: LCCN 2020001276 (print) | LCCN 2020001277 (ebook) |
ISBN 978-0-593-30275-0 (hardcover) | ISBN 978-0-593-12684-4 (library binding) |
ISBN 978-0-593-12685-1 (ebook)
Subjects: CYAC: Goal (Psychology)—Fiction. | Fortune cookies—Fiction. |
Best friends—Fiction. | Friendship—Fiction. | Family life—Fiction.
Classification: LCC PZ7.S9719 Ben 2021 (print) | LCC PZ7.S9719 (ebook) |
DDC [Fic]—dc23

ISBN 978-0-593-12683-7 (paperback)

Printed in the United States of America

10 9 8 7 6 5 4 3 2

First Yearling Edition 2022

To Batman,
for showing up exactly
when we needed you to

CHAPTER 1

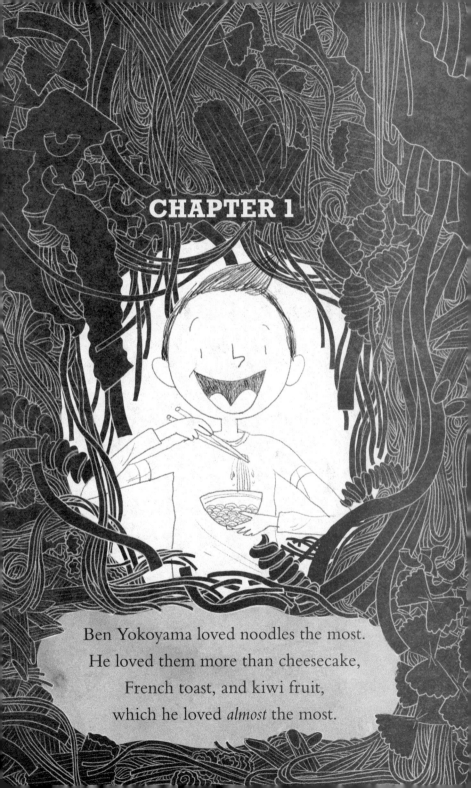

Ben Yokoyama loved noodles the most.
He loved them more than cheesecake,
French toast, and kiwi fruit,
which he loved *almost* the most.

He loved spaghetti noodles and udon noodles and tiny noodles shaped like stars. He loved thin noodles and wide noodles and round noodles and flat noodles. He loved any food with "noodle" in its name. Ben was a noodle man.

Are you ready to order?

asked his aunt Nora, looking up from her phone.

Ben was not ready to order. He'd never been to a Chinese restaurant. There were *so many options*.

His parents preferred the Japanese restaurant, but they were home paying three months of bills all at once. Nora was in charge tonight.

Do they have noodles?

Ben asked.

Yes, they have noodles,

said Nora like her brain was on one planet and her mouth was on another. "There," she said, pointing to a part of the menu that said NOODLES.

Aunt Nora had long fake fingernails on top of her regular ones. They tapped against her phone like rain on a roof. Ben wondered how hard it would be to open jars with fingernails like that.

He read the list of noodle dishes.

– Chow mein!

– Lo mein!

–Dandan!

Chow *fun!*

Ben wanted to eat a noodle that was fun!

Once he had decided what to order, Ben thought about what to do next. He considered writing a limerick or whistling "Clair de lune" or folding his place mat into an origami elephant.

But there was no rush. Ben was only eight years old. He had a whole wide lifetime to do these things. So instead, he sat patiently while Aunt Nora used her phone to take a picture of her menu.

By the time the waiter came, Ben had forgotten the name of the fun-sounding noodle and he couldn't find it again in the ocean of options.

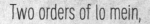

Two orders of lo mein,

said Aunt Nora. And then she went back to fiddling with her phone and not talking to Ben.

He didn't mind. The TV over her shoulder was showing great mountains of noodles being born in a noodle factory. It made the waiting difficult.

When the actual noodles
came, Ben ate them like a flame
eats a piece of paper when you throw
it in the fireplace. Lo mein wasn't
particularly fun, but it sure was delicious.

Nora ate six noodles. Ben knew because
he counted. He couldn't understand it.

"Are you going to eat the *rest* of your
noodles?" asked Ben once his noodles were gone.
But Aunt Nora didn't hear him. She was busy
taking a picture of her fingernails.

Ben felt sorry for Nora's noodles, sitting
there unloved.

Here, he said to the noodles,

I'll make you feel better.

Ben took Nora's plate and ate her
noodles like an anteater eats ants. He was
sad that his stomach was not infinite.

The waiter took their plates away and brought a tiny tray that held two little lumps wrapped in plastic. They looked like dried-out ravioli, which was another kind of noodle Ben loved.

What *are* they?

he asked.

Fortune cookies,

said Nora.

They're full of wisdom.

Ben was a big
fan of wisdom.

Nora split her cookie in two, pulled out
a tiny strip of paper, and read out loud.

Be sure to notice the wonders that surround you, or else you might miss them.

That's good advice,

said Ben.

It really is,

said Nora, placing the strip of paper on the tiny plate and taking a picture with her phone.

Ben split his cookie in two and found his own strip of paper inside.

Here's what it said:

Live each day as if

it were your last.

Oh boy,

said Ben, his mind devouring the wisdom
like a black hole devours planets and stars.

9

Live each day as if

CHAPTER 2

Ben thought about his

He thought about it as he walked past the dining

He thought about it as he brushed his teeth,

And then he dreamed about it.

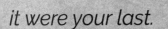

it were your last.

fortune all the way home.

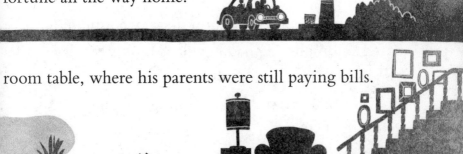

room table, where his parents were still paying bills.

put on his pajamas, and got into bed.

Everything was different now.
Suddenly a lifetime had become a single day.

CHAPTER 3

Ben's alarm clock woke him up at one minute after midnight. He had big plans for his last day and wanted to get started as early as possible.

But Ben was not used to being up quite so early. He preferred to sleep in on Saturday mornings. As much as he wanted to leap out of bed, his body refused to cooperate.

This is awful, he thought. He heard himself think it, and he agreed.

But, he thought next, *if today is the last day of my life, I don't want to waste more than one minute of it being asleep.*

Ben got out of bed. He jumped up and down a few times to wake himself up. It helped. He went to the bathroom and put his face in the sink and turned the cold water on. That helped even more. Ben was awake.

Then he went to the kitchen and drank a glass of orange juice and read his fortune for the fourteenth time.

Live each day as if it were your last.

This is great advice, thought Ben. *But how do I do it?*

There was no one to tell Ben what to do, so instead he told himself.

I need to do all the things I've always wanted to do! thought Ben, standing up to show himself he meant it. *But what are those things?* he thought next, sitting down again because he wasn't quite sure.

I need to make a list, Ben decided.

He got a piece of paper from the bin that said PAPER and a pencil from the jar that said PENCILS. Ben's dad liked to label things.

One of Ben's goals for any day, not just his *last* day but *every single day*, was to eat a piece of cake.

Ben started a list.

Ben looked at his list. It wasn't long, but it was already perfect.

What else? he wondered.

But Ben was so interested in the first item on his list that he was having trouble coming up with a second.

He remembered something
interesting and opened the
freezer. There, behind the pork
chops and the peas, was a big piece
of cake wrapped in plastic. Taped
to the cake was a note that said:

DO NOT EAT
THIS CAKE.

The word "not" was underlined twice.

Ben had seen the cake before and had never
been tempted to eat it because of the note, which
he knew from the handwriting had been written
by his dad.

But things were different now. This could be
his *last day*. Surely his dad would not mind if Ben
ate the forbidden cake on what could be the *last
day of his life!*

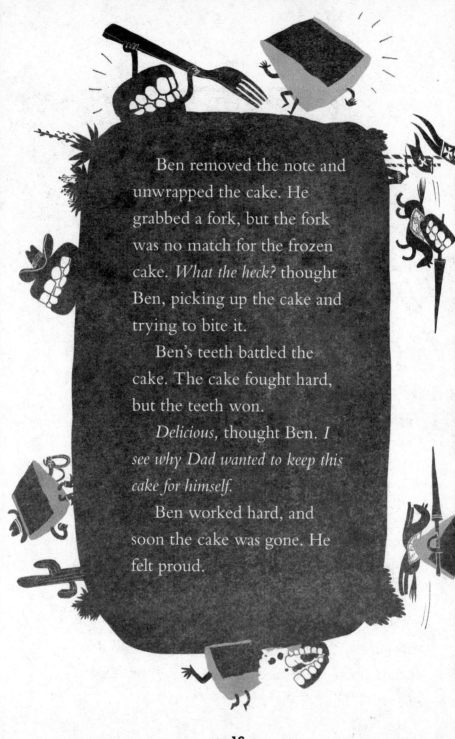

Ben removed the note and unwrapped the cake. He grabbed a fork, but the fork was no match for the frozen cake. *What the heck?* thought Ben, picking up the cake and trying to bite it.

Ben's teeth battled the cake. The cake fought hard, but the teeth won.

Delicious, thought Ben. *I see why Dad wanted to keep this cake for himself.*

Ben worked hard, and soon the cake was gone. He felt proud.

He looked at his list and his pencil.

• Eat a piece of cake

This is going so well,

he thought.

CHAPTER 4

What's next? Ben wondered.

He thought and thought. And as he did, he scribbled.

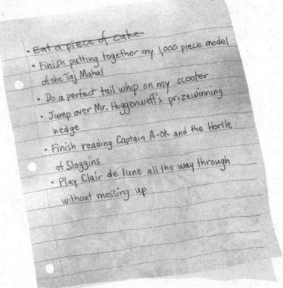

- Eat a piece of cake
- Finish putting together my 1,000 piece model of the Taj Mahal
- Do a perfect tail whip on my scooter
- Jump over Mr. Hoggenweff's prizewinning hedge
- Finish reading Captain A-ok and the Hortle of Sloggins
- Play Clair de lune all the way through without messing up

It was a pretty good list. But maybe not a *perfect* list. Ben wanted to add something big, like *Learn to speak Japanese,* but he knew it probably wouldn't be possible in just one day.

Ben needed his best friend, Janet. Janet thought big. But it was the middle of the night, and she was probably asleep.

Ben tried to think big like Janet, but his thoughts remained small.

I wonder how she does it? he wondered.

Ben tried again. A great big thought came into his head like an elephant coming into your tree house. He added it to his list.

Eat a whole cake at once

Ben smiled. Janet would be proud. He didn't know if the thought was even possible, but it was definitely big.

Ben's list was getting long. It was time to get started.

The Taj Mahal was an extremely complicated building in India. The model had been a gift from Ben's aunt Mindy, who was Aunt Nora's twin sister but had regular fingernails and an old-fashioned phone with no camera.

Ben spread the thousand pieces on the living room floor, just like he had seven times before. But just like the other seven times, Ben needed glue to stick them together.

And just like the other seven times, the glue was not where it was supposed to be.

Ben knew he had used the glue recently, but *where, where, where?*

Ben thought and thought. He remembered his dad saying,

Don't forget to put the glue away, Ben. You have to start taking responsibility for your own belongings, Ben.

Ben remembered saying, *I will!* and stomping out of the room.

But *which* room?

Ben remembered!

He had been doing a science experiment in the back of his parents' bedroom closet.

But it was impossible to get to the closet without first going into his parents' bedroom. Which was where his parents were currently sleeping.

Normally, I would just wait and get the glue in the morning, thought Ben. *But since this could be the last day of my life, there isn't any time to waste.*

Ben went upstairs. Dumbles the dog was lying in front of his parents' bedroom door. Exactly and completely in front. It was impossible to open the door without first convincing Dumbles to move.

Ben tugged on Dumbles's leg. He pushed him gently. It was no use. Dumbles was like a tiny hippopotamus.

Ben went down to the fridge to find some ham. But there was no ham. No turkey. No roast beef. There was only tofu. Ben's dad loved tofu.

Ben put tofu right in front of Dumbles's nose.

Here you go, Dumby,

he said.

Delicious, *scrumptious tofu!*

Ben did his best to make the tofu sound exciting.

Dumbles opened one eye and gave a bored sniff before turning his head in the other direction and closing the eye again.

This made sense to Ben. Dumbles was his mom's dog, really. And his mom was not a fan of tofu.

Ben had a better idea. He
went down to the kitchen and
filled Dumbles's water bowl.

Then he brought it back upstairs
and set it down in front of Dumbles, who
wouldn't even open the one eye this time.

Ben had a *better* better idea. He went
downstairs, filled Dumbles's bowl with milk,
and added six squirts of strawberry syrup, which
made the milk pink and delicious.

Ben carried the bowl up the stairs and set it
down in front of Dumbles. Dumbles opened the
one eye again and glanced at the milk.

Dumbles wasn't sure.

Ben got a spoon and gave Dumbles a taste.

Dumbles smiled. Dumbles lifted his head. Dumbles drank that milk like a desert drinks a rainstorm.

Soon the milk was gone, and Dumbles lay down. But only for a second. Dumbles stood up. Which was exactly what Ben had hoped would happen.

Do you have to go outside, Dumbly Doo?

Dumbles gave Ben a look that said,

Yes, please, and right now, if you don't mind.

Ben let Dumbles out into the yard. He did not let Dumbles back in.

25

CHAPTER 5

Slowly and quietly Ben opened his parents'
bedroom door. His mom slept like a hibernating
bear, which is to say, flat on her back with a
pillow on her face. Ben's dad slept like a nervous
rabbit, which is to say, tossing and turning and
ready to start sprinting at the first sign of a fox.

Lucky for Ben, his parents' bedroom floor was
covered with a soft and spongy carpet. Which
made it easy to creep over to the closet without
waking them.

The bedroom was dark. The closet was *darker*.

Ben tried to turn on his flashlight. But it
remained disappointingly *off*.

Drat, darn, and dang, thought Ben.

He remembered taking the batteries out of the flashlight and putting them into his walkie-talkie. *But where was his walkie-talkie?*

He remembered his dad saying, "You need to take responsibility for your walkie-talkie, Ben."

Ben couldn't remember where he had been standing when his dad said those words. His dad said those words so often, in so many different rooms.

Ben decided he didn't need a flashlight. He would find the glue in the dark. It would be like exploring a cave. A cave full of pants and shirts and shoes.

He was pretty sure he had been using the glue in the far back corner of the closet, trying to see whether it would be strong enough to glue two of his dad's shoes together.

Ben felt his way along the line of shoes. There were so many kinds. Smooth shoes, rough shoes, stinky shoes, and . . .

Shoes stuck together with glue!

Ben had found the glue! But there was a problem. The bottle containing the glue was stuck to the carpet.

Drat, darn, and dang!

said Ben, out loud this time.

Ben?

said Ben's dad like a panicky rabbit
who is suddenly wide awake.

CHAPTER 6

Ben yanked hard, and the glue came loose. He put it in his pocket.

"Is that you, Ben?" asked Ben's dad like a panicky rabbit who just found a fox in his closet.

UH-WOO-WOO-WOO-WO came a sound from the yard.

"What was that?" asked Ben's dad like a panicky rabbit who is suddenly more concerned about the werewolf outside.

"Dumbles, Dumbles," said Ben's mom like a hibernating bear who can't believe it's already spring.

"There must be an intruder!" gasped Ben's dad to no one but himself.

"Either in my dream or in the actual house. *I can't tell which!*"

Ben crept to the front of the closet and peeked into his parents' room. His dad was standing on the bed, clutching two pillows as if they were the only thing keeping him from floating into space.

Ben thought he might be able to just wait this out. Eventually, his dad would realize that the howling was just Dumbles and let him back in. Eventually, his dad would go back to bed. *Eventually.*

H-WOO-WOO-WOO-WOO

howled Dumbles again, but louder this time.

> I *must* be asleep,

said Ben's dad, climbing down from the bed and looking out the window.

> No *living* creature could make such a horrible sound! But if this is a dream, why can't I wake up?! La-la-la-la-la!

He kicked his legs and waved his arms, trying to dance himself awake.

Come on now,

said Ben's mom,
who was still asleep
but clearly not
happy with the way
things were going.

Ben felt bad. He stepped out of the closet.
"Everything's okay, Dad."
"Hi, Ben," said his dad with a grateful smile.
"I'm so glad you're here in my dream!"
"I'm not in your dream, Dad.
You're already awake."
Ben's dad looked relieved.
But then he looked worried.
"Then someone *is* trying
to break into our house. Or
some . . . *thing.* Maybe an extremely
disappointed walrus."

UH-WOO-WOO-WOO

No one's trying to break in. There is no walrus. I let Dumbles out, and I forgot to let him back in.

For a moment, Ben's dad looked relieved again. But then he looked confused.

What were you doing in our closet?

Just getting my glue.

Ben's dad looked at the clock by his bed.

At 1:13 in the morning?

I need it to put together my thousand-piece model of the Taj Mahal.

Ben's dad no longer looked confused. Now he just looked mad.

At 1:13 in the morning?!

Ben decided to just say it. "This could be *the last day of my life!*"

Now Ben's dad looked shocked and sad. He reached out to give Ben a hug. "What are you talking about? Of course it's not your last day! *You're only eight years old!*"

"I know!" said Ben. "That's what makes it so tragic."

"What makes you think it's your last day?"

"My fortune cookie said so."

Ben's dad looked relieved. "Fortune cookies are just for fun, Benny. This *isn't* your last day!"

Ben was not convinced.

But what if it *is*?

What *if*?

Ben's dad got a serious look as the wisdom of the cookie sank in. "I see what you mean," he said, sitting down on his bed like a sunset sits down on a mountain. "The planet could be smashed by an asteroid at any minute!"

"Or attacked by angry aliens!" said Ben.

"Exactly!" said Ben's dad. "Or . . . swallowed by a supernova."

His eyes grew wide and determined. "We have to make the most of this day!"

"I know!" said Ben. "I'm making a list of all the things I want to do."

"I will, too!" said Ben's dad, as awake and alert as a rooster at dawn. "Thank you, Ben!"

"You're welcome," said Ben.

"Uh-woo-woo-woo-woo," said Dumbles.

Ben's mom said nothing. All of the pillows were now on her head, and she seemed to be sound asleep.

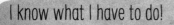

I know what I have to do!

said Ben's dad with a look like a person who's planning on climbing Mount Everest.

He put a sweater on over his pajamas and raced out of the room. A moment later, Ben heard the garage door open and watched out the window as the green car drove away.

Ben's dad was the greatest, but he sometimes did things that were hard to understand. Ben went downstairs and opened the door and let Dumbles inside.

He pulled out his copy of *Captain A-OK and the Hortle of Sloggins* and set it on the table in the living room next to the glue. He looked at the one thousand pieces of the Taj Mahal and rolled up his sleeves. It was what Captain A-OK always did when he had a lot to accomplish.

Ben had a lot to accomplish.

CHAPTER 7

Ben's mom woke him up by touching his cheeks and kissing his forehead.

What are you doing down here?

she asked with a smile.

Ben was on the couch in the living room. It was morning. On the table in front of the couch was the Taj Mahal. It was a little crooked, but all one thousand pieces were in place.

When did you do *that*?

All night long.

You stayed up all night long building your one-thousand-piece model of the Taj Mahal? *Why?*

Because, said Ben, pausing a bit to let his mom know that what he was about to say was extremely important, **this could be the last day of my life.**

Ben's mom gave Ben a funny look. "It *could* be, but I don't think that's very *likely*." She touched both of his cheeks and kissed his forehead again. "I certainly *hope* it isn't."

"Where's Dad?" asked Ben, wondering if the green car had ever come back.

"Still asleep," said Ben's mom with a puzzled expression. Ben's dad always got up first. "Paying those bills must have tired him out."

Then she went into the kitchen and banged pots together like she always did when Ben's dad wasn't there and she had to make breakfast by herself.

Ben looked at the Taj Mahal. He was proud. Then he saw his copy of *Captain A-OK*. He had read only a few pages of chapter six before falling asleep.

Ben walked over to the piano and tried playing "Clair de lune." He started out fine but messed up when things got faster in the middle. He tried again, but his fingers got tangled like a kite string in a rosebush.

It was the most beautiful song in the world, and he wanted to play it perfectly at least once in his life. Which meant he had some practicing to do.

UH-WOO-WOO

said Dumbles, who hated it
when Ben played the piano and
especially when he messed up
"Clair de lune."

Ben was about to try for a third time when
his mom walked into the room with a face as icy
as a flagpole in January.

What do you know about *this*?

She was holding something.
It was the note that said to not eat
the cake. Ben had meant to throw
the note away, but the rest of his
list had distracted him.

Ben was extremely disappointed in
himself.

His mom's face demanded an answer,
but Ben was having trouble finding the
courage to be entirely honest.

DO NOT EAT
THIS CAKE.

It looks like Dad's handwriting to me.

To me, too. Have you seen it before?

I've seen Dad's handwriting plenty of times. I like how he makes his K's.

I *do* like how he makes his K's,

said Ben's mom, smiling like a firefly lighting up in the dark. But then, like a firefly when it's finished, she suddenly stopped glowing.

But that is not the point, mister.

When Ben's mom called him "mister," it meant things were slipping from bad to so much worse.

It *isn't?*

asked Ben with a squeeze in his throat.

"It certainly is not. I assume this note *just happened* to fall out of the freezer, and that when I open the freezer, that piece of cake will still be there, because *no one I know* would read a note like this and then do the *exact opposite*."

With every word, Ben shrank an inch. By the time his mom was done talking, he was the size of a soda can that someone has flattened for recycling.

No one I know, either,

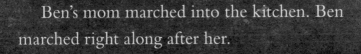

said Ben, searching through the various cabinets of his heart to see if he could find an extra can of courage.

Ben's mom marched into the kitchen. Ben marched right along after her.

Then she marched over to the freezer.

Maybe it was Aunt Nora.
Maybe she didn't see the note.

But Ben knew
Nora didn't like
cake, and Ben's
mom knew it, too.

That seems
pretty unlikely.

"Maybe Dad put it in a *different* freezer for safekeeping."

"Nope. Your dad trusts us, Ben. He knows no one in this family would eat his clearly labeled cake."

She grabbed the handle on the freezer door. The freezer door was about to open. It was Ben's very last chance to be brave, and he decided to take it.

I ate the cake,

he said as
loud and as
clear as he could
manage, which
wasn't very loud
or clear at all.

"Excuse me?" said Ben's mom in a voice like the small, sharp knife you use to cut apples.

"I ate it," said Ben, feeling worried but also relieved as the plain, true words tumbled out of his mouth. "I couldn't help myself."

"Oh, *Ben!*" said Ben's mom with her actually-sad-and-not-just-faking-it-to-make-a-point face. "How *could* you?"

Because . . . it could be the last day of my life.

This *isn't* the last day of your life, *mister,*

she said with her actually-mad-and-not-just-faking-it-to-be-funny face.

Stop saying that it is.

Ben could tell that his mom was *exasperated.* He knew because she made the face so often that one day he'd asked her what word he should use to describe it.

This is my exasperated face, she had told him at the time.

"I like that word," Ben had said. "It's a really good word."

"It *is* a good word," she had said, and because she was such a big fan of good words and was so glad that Ben was interested in learning them, she had gotten a lot *less* exasperated.

But that was that day, and this was this one.

On that day, Ben hadn't eaten a slice of forbidden cake. Today the exasperation was going to stick around for a while.

CHAPTER 8

Ben's dad walked into the kitchen with a
gigantic smile.

Good morning, sleepy bones,

said Ben's mom with a
gigantic smile of her own.

Don't make any plans for tonight.

All right,

she said with a face that meant, *Oh no,
what important date did I forget?*

Also . . . this is for you.

Ben's dad gave Ben's mom a purple flower
he'd been hiding behind his back.

Her *Oh no* face changed to her melting-rainbow face. "You shouldn't have," she said, but what she meant was, *You definitely should have, and I'm really glad you did.*

There was hugging and kissing, so Ben decided to fold some origami.

Then Ben's mom went off to do her morning things, but as she did, she glanced over at Ben with a face that meant, *Our conversation isn't over yet, mister.*

As soon as she was gone, Ben's dad turned to Ben and said,

Because it could be the last day of my life, I'm taking your mom out to dinner to celebrate our nine years, three months, and seventeen days anniversary.

He was bubbly like a pot of water right when it starts to boil.

Ben liked dinner. But he couldn't understand why his dad seemed so excited about this one. "Great," said Ben.

And then, remembering, he asked, "Where did you go in the middle of the night?"

"I went out to Whistling Reservoir and cleared away some bushes and weeds in the exact place where I asked your mom to marry me, so that I can take her there tonight after dinner and ask her to marry me again." Ben's dad looked proud, like he had just won a karate tournament.

Ben had so many questions.

"You cleared away bushes and weeds?"

"It wasn't so bad. The ground was soft. It had recently rained."

Ben noticed that his dad's hands were kind of green.

"In the middle of the night?"

"It could be the last day of my life! There was no time to waste."

Ben agreed with that part.

"Why would you need to marry Mom . . . again?"

"I don't *need* to. I just *want* to."

That made no sense to Ben, either, but it clearly made a lot of sense to his dad, who continued to tell Ben the many details of what he and Ben's mom had eaten for dinner and dessert at an Italian restaurant called Luna Lupa on the night they got engaged.

While Ben's dad was talking, Ben's brain wandered off to think about what else he should add to his list.

But his dad was not done.

"And . . . as a surprise for your mom, I'm going to bring along the leftover piece of our wedding cake that I've been saving in the freezer for our ten-year anniversary! Because if this is the last day of my life, I'd hate to miss the chance to eat it."

All of a sudden, Ben's brain came sprinting right back.

CHAPTER 9

Ben's dad went off to take a shower, and his mom came back to the kitchen.

Ben was torn. His dad had told him a secret, and his mom always said that keeping someone's secret was extremely important.

But then Ben thought about what might happen when his dad discovered that the cake was missing.

Ben's mom *also* always said that sometimes you have to make difficult decisions.

Ben made a decision. It was difficult.

He told his mom about his dad's cake plans.

First she said, "Aww . . . ," and then she said, *"BEN!"* and then she said, "What are we going to *do*?"

It was like being at the beach on a day with complicated weather.

Eventually, Ben's mom settled into what Ben called her "determined" face, which was also the face she used when making pancakes or doing three months of bills all at once.

"People bake cakes all the time," said Ben's mom, but what she really meant was, *I have no idea how to bake a cake.*

"They use ingredients and follow recipes, and at the end there is a cake," she said next. But what she really meant was, *I am a successful and self-confident person, but the idea of baking a cake makes me want to scream.*

"Do you want to scream?" Ben asked.

said Ben's mom, her determined face collapsing for just a moment into her extremely frustrated one.

But then she stood up tall and said in a clear, strong voice that made Ben believe she meant it,

No, Ben, I do not want to scream. I want to make a blueberry-lemon buttermilk chiffon cake with Italian buttercream frosting.

Will you help me?

Yes!

Ben liked his mom's triumphant face best of all.

"Great," said Ben's mom. "But first we've got to get your dad out of the house."

"Right," said Ben. "But how?"

"Watch the master," she said. *"Ken,"* she called out in a voice that sounded almost like a lullaby.

"Yes?" said Ben's dad, walking into the room with wet hair and a smile you might use on the first day of summer vacation. (Ben's dad took really quick showers.) Ben was glad that his dad's last day seemed to be going so well. He was determined to keep it that way.

Ben's mom smiled at his dad, and his dad smiled back. She kept smiling like they were having a contest to see who could smile longest. (Ben's mom always won those kinds of contests.)

"I've been thinking," she said, "and if today really is the *last day of my life,* what I *really* want is some double fudge banana frost ice cream."

"The kind we had on our very first date!" said Ben's dad, as gleeful as if he were watching a parade of baby otters in tiny tuxedos.

Exactly.

But that was in—

West Bomford.

Unfortunately, I think they only make it and sell it in—

West Bomford.

But West Bomford is—

Three hours away, and only if you drive really fast.

Ben's dad was making his *But we really need to finish paying the three months of bills today* face. "I would do it in a second, but . . ."

"But it could be . . . ," said Ben's mom with her *See how sad I am?* face.

"The last day of your *life*," said Ben's dad, the sad look warming his heart like a blowtorch warms an ice cube. "I know what I have to do!"

Ben's dad grabbed the keys and marched out into the garage. He drove the green car away.

Ben's mom looked at Ben. Her determined face was back.

"Okay," she said, "We have six hours. I'm going to Near Alfredo's for blueberries and lemons. You stay here and vacuum the living room."

There were two Alfredo's supermarkets in town. One was nearby. The other was extremely far away.

Okay,

said Ben.

His mom took the blue car and left.

Ben *wanted* to vacuum the living room. He really did. But because it was possibly the last day of Janet's life, too, he had to let her know as soon as possible.

CHAPTER 10

Janet lived in the house behind Ben's, but there was an extremely tall fence between their yards.

He could have ridden his scooter all the way around the block. Instead, he climbed the oak tree in his yard, wiggled himself along the limb that reached out over the fence, and dropped down onto Janet's trampoline. This way was much faster.

To get back home, Ben would have to go the whole way around the block. Janet's yard lacked an oak tree.

Ben let himself in the back door and found Janet reading comics in the middle of her living-room floor.

He didn't know how to break the bad news, so he decided to ease into it.

"Imagine it's my last day," he said.

Janet looked concerned.

Are you sick? She put her hand on his forehead and frowned.

You don't *feel* sick, and you don't *look* sick.

I'm not sick. But my fortune cookie said it could be my last day. So I have to assume that it might be.

"It's *not* your last day," said Janet, who was as practical as a socket wrench. "A fortune is just a piece of paper that someone shoved into a cookie. *Anyone* could have gotten that fortune."

But *I* did.

"It's *not* your last day," said Janet with as much certainty as an art teacher says *Yellow and blue make green*.

"But what if it *is*?" Ben insisted.

Janet looked as puzzled as someone who had just learned the right way to spell "rendezvous."

"Yes. I see what you mean," she said, her face twisting itself from a breadstick into a pretzel. "What if it is *my* last day?" Suddenly Janet seemed anything but practical.

"Exactly," said Ben, who felt understood. "How would you spend it?" he prompted, eagerly waiting for big thoughts to come.

He didn't have to wait long.

I would eat a lot of pancakes. It's important to eat the things you love most on your last day of life.

"I completely agree," said Ben, remembering why he and Janet were such good friends. "Do you happen to have an entire cake?"

"Nope," said Janet, who didn't seem surprised by the question. She knew Ben pretty well.

How about a whole box of spaghetti, then?

he asked.

Janet marched to the kitchen and opened the pantry. She pulled out a box of spaghetti, a jar of spaghetti sauce, and a box of pancake mix.

Ben's eyes got
as big as
marshmallows
in a microwave.

Then they got
narrow like
fingernail
clippings.

"Is your mom home?"

"She's at work."

Janet's mom was a librarian who had to work on Saturdays. Ben knew better than to ask about Janet's dad.

"And we're not allowed to use the stove?"

"No, sir."

Ben was discouraged. He liked noodles because they were slippery and soft. "Shucks."

"Shucks, what?" asked Janet.

"Shucks, I wanted to eat a whole box of spaghetti, but now I can't."

"Who says you can't?"

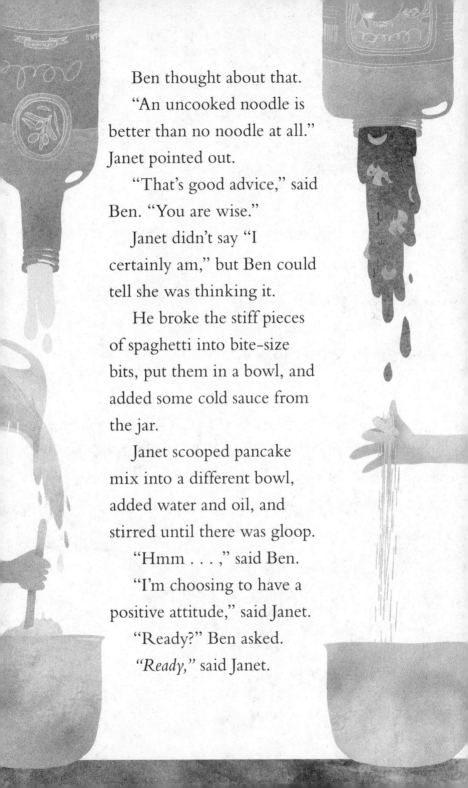

Ben thought about that.

"An uncooked noodle is better than no noodle at all." Janet pointed out.

"That's good advice," said Ben. "You are wise."

Janet didn't say "I certainly am," but Ben could tell she was thinking it.

He broke the stiff pieces of spaghetti into bite-size bits, put them in a bowl, and added some cold sauce from the jar.

Janet scooped pancake mix into a different bowl, added water and oil, and stirred until there was gloop.

"Hmm . . . ," said Ben.

"I'm choosing to have a positive attitude," said Janet.

"Ready?" Ben asked.

"Ready," said Janet.

They were quiet for a moment as Ben chewed
his crunchy noodle bits and Janet slurped her gloop.

Janet opened her mouth as if she were about to say another big, wise thing.

But then she stopped, as if she knew that it was actually a *terrible* idea.

"Say it!" said Ben.

At first Janet didn't say it. But then she did.

CHAPTER 11

"Marshmallows don't need to be cooked," said Janet.

"More wisdom!" said Ben, who had forgotten all about their sworn pledge to each eat an entire bag of marshmallows as soon as they turned eighteen and were free to be as foolish as they wanted to.

Ben saw what Janet was thinking. They were not eighteen. Not even close.

"But if this is the last day of our lives . . . ," said Janet.

"Then we pretty much *have* to," said Ben.

They went to the cupboard. There were three full bags of marshmallows. The *big* kind.

"I'm so happy about this," said Ben.

"It was meant to be," said Janet.

They both took a
bag. Ben stuffed seven
marshmallows into his
mouth. Janet stuffed
eleven into hers. Ben
chewed and chewed. It
was so wonderful he
wanted to cry.

It's so wonderful
I want to cry,

said Janet once she
was done chewing.

Ben wanted to agree, but his mouth was
already full of nine more marshmallows. It took
about five minutes, but soon they were both
holding empty bags and feeling extremely
energetic.

"What else?" Janet asked.

Ben thought big. Suddenly *anything* seemed
possible.

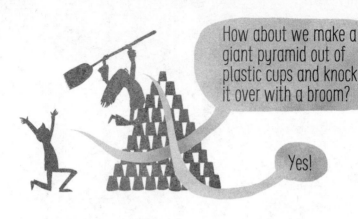

How about we make a giant pyramid out of plastic cups and knock it over with a broom?

Yes!

They did it. It was thrilling.

"How about we stack all the sofa cushions on top of each other and see if we can touch the ceiling?" Janet proposed.

They did it. It was wobbly and maybe a little bit dangerous, but they *did* touch the ceiling.

Then they blew up a full pack of balloons and popped them one by one, broke a full bag of baby carrots in half, and tried on most of Janet's mom's hats.

Just as they were running out of ideas, Ben had a new one. "Operation Catapult?"

"Yes!"

They went out to the trampoline.

They had figured out that if one person bounced down  just as the other person was about to bounce up, *the person going up would spring much higher.*

Maybe even high enough to grab on to the big branch and make it back to Ben's yard without having to walk around the block.

If they timed it perfectly.

They had been trying for weeks but hadn't made it work. *Yet.*

"It's now or never,"
said Ben.

They bounced and bounced.
Ben timed his landing perfectly, and
Janet got pretty close to reaching the
branch.

Then Janet timed her landing
perfectly, and Ben got even closer.

But no matter how perfectly they
timed it, they couldn't get *quite* high
enough.

So they bounced just to bounce
for a while.

At the highest part of each
bounce, they had an excellent view
of Ben's yard and the other yards
along the block.

"Oh," said Janet. "I remember
something else I've always wanted to
do."

Janet landed just as Ben was about to
take off, sending him high into the air.

"What?" he asked.

"I want to eat an apple
from Mrs. Ezra's tree."

Mrs. Ezra lived on Ben's side of the block, two
houses down from his. She was very old and
extremely mysterious. At night, she burned
candles instead of turning on lamps. She always
wore hats, even when it wasn't cold. Instead
of using her front door, she always used
the one on the side of her house.
*As if she had something
to hide!*

In the center of Mrs. Ezra's yard was
a magnificent old apple tree with apples
that looked impossibly delicious. Ben
had always wanted to taste them and
had even thought about sneaking over
the fence to get one. But he never
had. For obvious reasons.

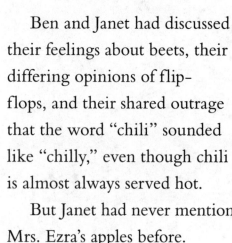

Ben and Janet had discussed their feelings about beets, their differing opinions of flip-flops, and their shared outrage that the word "chili" sounded like "chilly," even though chili is almost always served hot.

But Janet had never mentioned Mrs. Ezra's apples before.

I've heard they're enchanted,

said Janet without explanation, forcing Ben to ask,

What do you mean?

I mean, they have magical powers. If you eat them, amazing things happen.

Like what?

Ben had heard rumors about Mrs. Ezra being more than just strange, but hearing them from Janet made him especially worried. She was not the type to make things up.

"Wow," said Ben. He was excited. Eating an enchanted apple from the tree of an actual witch was definitely a big idea.

How are you going to get one?

Ben couldn't wait to hear Janet's plan.

I'm not.

What do you mean?

I mean, it's too risky. If a panther takes my cupcake, I'm not going to argue about it. I'm going to let the panther have my cupcake.

Why are we talking about panthers?

We're not. That was just an example. We're still talking about enchanted apples. The point is, if this is my last day, I definitely don't want to spend it as a troll.

But if you *don't* get the apple today, you might never know what it tastes like!

Life is full of tough decisions, Ben.

Ben supposed that was true.
But he didn't have to like it.

They bounced a bit
longer. "I'm beat," said
Janet. "Let's go inside."
"Sounds good," said Ben,
who was getting tired, too.

As Janet took her final bounce, Ben
saw her glance longingly over the fence
at Mrs. Ezra's yard. Which made him
wonder whether occasionally it *did* made
sense to take a cupcake from a panther.
What good is a big idea, thought Ben,
without an equally big plan to bring it to life?

CHAPTER 12

They went back inside and sat side by side on the big blue chair, exhausted but delighted.

"Are we done?" asked Ben. "Is there anything left?"

"Hmm," said Janet.

Ben could see another big thought brewing.

Oh, said Janet, with a look that was big but also sad.

What? asked Ben. He was worried.

I just remembered something I absolutely *have* to do if this is my last day.

What is it?

Janet didn't answer. Instead, she popped up from the chair and marched upstairs.

Ben marched right behind her.

She walked down the hall to her bedroom, opened her bottom dresser drawer, and pulled out a stack of the most unfortunate sweaters Ben had ever seen.

"Aunt Lupita made them," Janet explained when she saw Ben's face. "I have to keep them for when she visits. Luckily, that doesn't happen very often."

"Is she visiting today?"

"She's not," said Janet, who was acting like her mind was orbiting a planet that was dingy and damp.

Next, Janet pulled out a bag that contained some sort of craft project. Ben saw yarn and a pattern and a very strange tool.

"What's all that?"

Janet sat on the floor and opened the bag. "A latch hook rug kit."

Ben had heard of latch hook rugs but had never actually seen one.

"Wow," he said, instead of saying, *This is strange and entirely unexpected.* Janet had never seemed like the crafty sort.

"Wow, what?"

"Wow, I didn't know you did latch hook," said Ben. It was a true statement.

"I don't," said Janet, the way a person might say, *It wasn't me,* when it's clear that someone in the room has tooted.

Ben was confused and didn't know what to say. Luckily, Janet kept talking.

I mean, I don't do latch hook very *often* because I don't particularly *enjoy it,*

she said with the weary expression of someone who has been treading water for fifteen minutes and is starting to sink.

Ben was baffled.

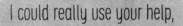

But this could be the last day of your life! Why would
you spend it doing something you don't—?

I could really use your help,

said Janet before
Ben could finish
his question.

There's still a
long way to go.

Ben looked at the rug. Maybe a third of it
was done.

"You need to finish it *today*?"

"I do," said Janet with her *We'd get done a lot
faster if you'd stop asking questions and start helping* face.

"How does it work?" Ben asked.

Janet showed him how to use a strange little
hook on a handle to attach a piece of
yarn to a stiff grid that was kind of
like a window screen.

"Here's a picture of what it will look like," said Janet, holding up a piece of paper that showed a bouquet of blue flowers in a bright orange vase. "Forget-me-nots."

Janet made a face like she'd recently cut an onion, but she swallowed hard and kept going.

"And here's the key." Janet held up a different piece of paper with a grid of tiny squares arranged in the shape of the rug. The squares contained letters. "*Y* is for yellow, *B* is for blue, *G* is for green, *BR* is for brown, and so on. That's how you know which color to use."

"Makes sense," said Ben.

"I'll start on this side and you start on that side, and with any luck we'll finish by the time my mom gets home."

It wasn't hard. It was actually kind of fun. Ben was really getting the hang of it when he saw something terrible through Janet's bedroom window.

CHAPTER 13

What Ben saw was the blue car.

It was driving down Janet's street. Which meant it would soon turn left and then left again before driving down Ben's street. And then it would park in Ben's driveway, which led to the garage, which was attached to a house that contained a living room that had not been vacuumed.

Ben needed to get home. *Fast.*

Janet understood.

"Go," she said. "I've got this."

Ben looked down at the rug. They had made a good start, but there were so many squares left to fill. "I'll come back as soon as I can."

"Thanks," said Janet. "Now *go!*"

Ben went. He thought about how close his house actually was, right on the other side of the fence. More than ever before, he blamed Janet's yard for not having an oak tree. He had no choice but to go all the way around the block.

And so Ben ran. He ran by the blue house that belonged to the Littles and the yellow house that had been for sale for a really long time. Ahead was the orange house that belonged to Mr. Hoggenweff, who had once won a prize for having a hedge that was perfectly rectangular. Mr. Hoggenweff was extremely proud of it.

Ben thought about his list.

- Jump over Mr. Hoggenweff's prizewinning hedge

Ben thought about the hedge as he ran. It was not especially tall. Nor was it particularly short. It was pretty much the perfect height for a satisfying challenge.

Ben was an excellent jumper.

He had already jumped over a large dog and a medium-size mountain bike and an extremely small pony.

Mr. Hoggenweff's hedge would probably be the highest thing he had ever jumped over, but Ben had no doubt that he could do it. In fact, he was *sure* he could.

The only reason he hadn't done it already was that Mr. Hoggenweff was almost always standing in his yard scowling, and Mr. Hoggenweff's scowl was a thing worse than nightmares.

But as Ben approached the orange house, it seemed like the coast was clear. Mr. Hoggenweff was nowhere to be seen.

So Ben changed course and headed straight for the hedge. He broke into an all-out sprint.

This is big, thought Ben. *This is the moment I've been waiting for.*

He was just a few feet from the hedge when Mr. Hoggenweff stepped out from behind a tall, flowering bush, holding a watering can.

His grouchy cat, Lovely, was standing there beside him, scowling.

EEEYAAGHA! Ben yelped.

It was not a brave sound.

Heeeeeyyyyy . . . there, Mr. Hoggenweff,

he said next, doing his best to sound calm and under control as he changed course without breaking his stride and, instead of leaping over the prizewinning hedge, ran right past it.

Mr. Hoggenweff never stopped
scowling as his eyes traced
Ben's path across the yard
and down the block.
When he rounded the
corner, Ben stopped
and took a deep
breath. He felt like
someone who had
just outrun
a tornado.

I am lucky to be alive! thought Ben. *Who knew my last day would be so dangerous?*

Ben took out his list.

- Jump over Mr. Hoggenweff's prizewinning hedge

Ben thought about erasing it. There was no rule that he had to finish *everything* on his list. But he decided not to give up. There was still so much of his last day left.

Which reminded him. The blue car! Ben started to sprint. The only scowl worse than Mr. Hoggenweff's belonged to his mom.

CHAPTER 14

When Ben got home, the blue car was already parked in the driveway. But Ben's mom didn't seem to notice that he was sweaty and out of breath. She was standing in the kitchen with her hands against the counter, as if it were the only thing holding her up.

Her face was a mixture of sad and mad and puzzled and tired and discouraged. Ben wanted to ask for the word to describe a face like that, but he was afraid it would be too difficult to pronounce.

Hi, Mom. How's it going?

Not well, Ben. Not well at all.

Ben figured his mom was upset that the living room floor was still covered in crumbs, dust, and tiny bits of Taj Mahal. But that wasn't it.

She was upset because she was reading a recipe and didn't like what it had to say.

"Great–Aunt Marie is not here, Ben."

Ben knew this was true but didn't know why his mom felt like pointing it out.

"Great–Aunt Marie is the one who made the blueberry-lemon buttermilk chiffon cake with Italian buttercream frosting for our wedding. Great–Aunt Marie knew what it meant to *clabber* the milk and to *fold* the egg whites into the batter. But I, for one, do not. Eggs are not a piece of paper, Ben!" She was getting pretty worked up.

How am I supposed to *fold* them? And what does it mean to *separate* the eggs? Am I supposed to put them in another room?

Ben's mom knew pretty much everything, and she really didn't like it when she stubbed her toe against something that she *didn't*.

Ben put his hand on her arm and led her to a chair.

I don't know what any of these things mean,

he said. He had never baked any cake, let alone a cake with a really long name.

But if we put our heads together, I know we can figure it out.

It was the sort of thing Ben's mom usually said to *him*, and he liked hearing the words come out of his own mouth instead.

His mom smiled and stood up.

Of *course* we can.

Ben used the internet to
find out that "clabbering" milk
just meant adding a little vinegar.

And that "folding" the egg
whites meant gently mixing them
into the batter once they had been
whipped into a fluffy froth.

"Then why don't they just *say* that?" Ben's
mom complained, switching to the exasperated
face that Ben much preferred to her discouraged
one.

"Apparently, 'separating' the eggs just means
putting the yolks in one bowl and the whites in
another."

"How are we
supposed to do *that*?!"
asked Ben's mom, as if
the recipe had
suggested they
swallow a porcupine.

"I'm pretty sure I
can do it."

Ben tried his best. Most of the yolks ended up in one bowl, and *most* of the whites ended up in another. And not *many* little jagged bits of shell got mixed in with them.

He only let *two or three* eggs roll off the counter and land on the floor with a splat. Dumbles was all too eager to help with the mess.

"It says we need some baking powder," said Ben.

"Is baking *powder* different from baking *soda*?" His mom was looking in the cabinet with the spices and such. "We have baking soda. And it's also white."

Ben assumed there *was* a difference and that the difference was *important*. But he didn't know for *sure*. "How different can they be?"

"Exactly," said Ben's mom with a look of relief.

They did all the things the recipe demanded. They mixed the flour, sugar, baking soda, and salt. They added the egg yolks, lemon juice, and oil.

It was time to mix the egg whites. "It says we need some cream of tartar," said Ben.

His mom rooted through the cabinet again.

"No luck," she said. "But we have some tartar sauce left over from Fish Stick Tuesday. Do you think that would work?"

Ben liked tartar sauce but couldn't imagine how a sauce full of pickles and mayonnaise would improve the taste of a *cake*. Especially pickles and mayonnaise that were already four days old. But his mom's pleading eyes made perfectly clear what she wanted the answer to be.

"I'm sure it will be fine," said Ben. It was the least true thing he'd said all week.

Ben mixed the egg whites and tartar sauce together, but they never turned into a fluffy froth. He tried his best to gently fold the runny, lumpy, pickly mess into the rest of the batter, which made it look bad and smell even worse.

"This is going so well!" said Ben.

"We are baking a cake!" said his mom like she needed a pep talk and was giving herself one.

They slid the pan into the oven and set a timer.

Ben's mom took a deep breath. "I need to sit down for a second," she said.

To Ben, it felt like they had just run ten miles on a bumpy road while performing open-heart surgery. He took a deep breath, too.

And then he realized. Even though making the cake had been complicated and confusing and uncertain, it had also been . . . fun.

Since his mom hated baking cakes, Ben had never baked a cake with his mom. Which is why he'd never known that baking a cake with his mom was something he wanted to do.

Which is why it wasn't on his list.

Yet.

Ben took out his list.

Bake a cake with Mom

He counted to ten, and then he crossed it out.

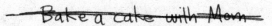

CHAPTER 15

While the cake baked, Ben and his mom sat next to the Taj Mahal and played a card game called *Whoops!* While they played *Whoops!*, Ben's mom looked at the floor and said,

So . . . Ben. This doesn't look like a floor that somebody vacuumed.

How did it get dirty again so quickly?

said Ben, trying to sound outraged.

Ben's mom gave him her *I see what you're up to* face, and Ben gave her his *But you can't stay mad at me for long when I make this face* face.

Ben's face was right.

It was impossible to argue after everything they'd just been through with the clabbering and the tartar sauce.

Ben vacuumed while his mom straightened the stack of magazines and turned the upside-down books upside up. When they were done, there were three minutes left on the timer, so they sat in front of the oven and hoped.

When the timer dinged, they took out the cake. It looked a lot like Janet's bowl of gloopy pancakes and smelled a lot like Ben's dad's jogging socks.

Ben looked at his mom. Her face was full of words that weren't okay to say out loud.

I'd like to curl up in the corner and cry, Ben.

But you're not going to, right?

No way! We're going to solve this problem, or my name's not Linda Yokoyama.

But her name *was* Linda Yokoyama.

Because that's what we do?

Because that, said Ben's mom, washing her hands and drying them on her pants, is what we do.

What next? asked Ben, who liked how his mom always seemed to know the answer to that question.

Plan B.

I'm going to the store to *buy* a cake. They didn't have a blueberry-lemon buttermilk chiffon cake with Italian buttercream frosting at *Near* Alfredo's, but maybe they'll have one at *Far* Alfredo's.

Ben gasped. "But Far
Alfredo's is . . ."

"I know," said Ben's mom.
Her face was grim. "But I see
no other choice."

Ben's mom grabbed the
keys to the blue car
and was just about to
leave when she said,

I thought of something you can do while I'm gone.

This was bad news. Ben had been planning to
go help Janet with her rug.

"Am I going to like it?" he asked, even
though he already knew the answer.

"You'll like it the same way you like spinach."

"I don't like spinach at all."

"Yes, but . . . ?"

"Spinach is good for me?"

"Exactly."

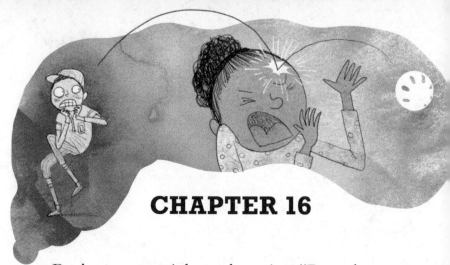

CHAPTER 16

Ben's mom got right to the point. "Does the name *Mona* ring a bell?"

She was not talking about an actual bell. She was talking about the bell that might ring in your head if someone said the name *Mona* and you had recently bonked someone named *Mona* in the head with a Wiffle ball.

Hmmm, said Ben, who remembered the moment well but preferred to pretend that he didn't.

Ben and his mom had recently had a long conversation about the importance of saying sorry, even if the Wiffle ball bonking was an accident, which it absolutely had been.

Ben was *working* on wanting to say sorry. "Maybe I'll apologize to Mona tomorrow."

"Usually that would be okay," said his mom, "but . . . since this might be the last day of your life . . ."

I'm pretty sure it isn't,

said Ben, suddenly convinced he would live another hundred years.

"But if it *were*," said his mom, "I bet it would be a *little easier* to say sorry on your last day than it might otherwise be."

Ben knew his mom was right. She almost always was.

"Okay," he said. "I'll do it."

"Great," she said. "But . . ."

"But?" Ben felt dread. His mom was famous for asking for something and then adding a "but."

"But it has to be a *good* apology. The kind that makes Mona actually *want* to forgive you."

"Okay," said Ben, trying to scoot out the door before another "but" showed up.

MES MOM
AS RIGHT

It was cold outside. Y☑ NO☐
. I shouldn't have
  eaten the 17ᵗʰ cookie. Y☑ NO☐
3. Dumbles didn't want
   to wear that sweater Y☑ NO☐
4. Dad's camera isn't
   waterproof. Y☑ NO☐
. x7 really does = 42 ☑ NO☐

Ben,

said his mom like a
rope that's attached to
your ankle.

Yes?

I'll know whether it's
a good apology or not.

I'll know.

Ben's mom always seemed to know the truth
of things, no matter how sneaky Ben was. He
had pretty much given up trying to be sneaky.
Pretty much.

"It will be the best apology Mona has ever
heard."

"I know it will," said Ben's mom with a grin.
"Good luck."

She got into the blue car and drove away.

Ben took out his list and added three words.

Apologize to Mona

Ben looked forward to apologizing to Mona about as much as a nail looks forward to getting hammered into a piece of wood. But he decided to do it anyway. For his mom. For his list. Because it was the right thing to do. He grabbed his scooter and rode it around the block to Mona's house, which was just a few doors down from Janet's.

I will apologize quickly, thought Ben, and then I will help Janet.

Ben felt like he was walking into the doctor's office. Apologizing was getting a shot. Helping Janet was the lollipop the nurse gives you afterward.

Ben leaned his scooter against a tree and knocked on Mona's door.

"Hi, Ben," said Mona's mom with the look that a fork might give a slice of pie.

"Hi, Mona's mom," said Ben.

"Diane," said Mona's mom. "You may call me *Diane*."

Diane had made this offer several times before, and Ben still wasn't ready to take her up on it. But he also had a feeling that things would go better if he did exactly as he was told.

"Hi, Diane," said Ben. "Is Mona here?"

"Did you bring your Wiffle ball?" asked Mona's mom, Diane, accusingly. "Is my daughter *safe*?"

Ben lifted his hands to show that they were empty. He gave a toothy smile to make clear that he had nothing dangerous hidden in his mouth.

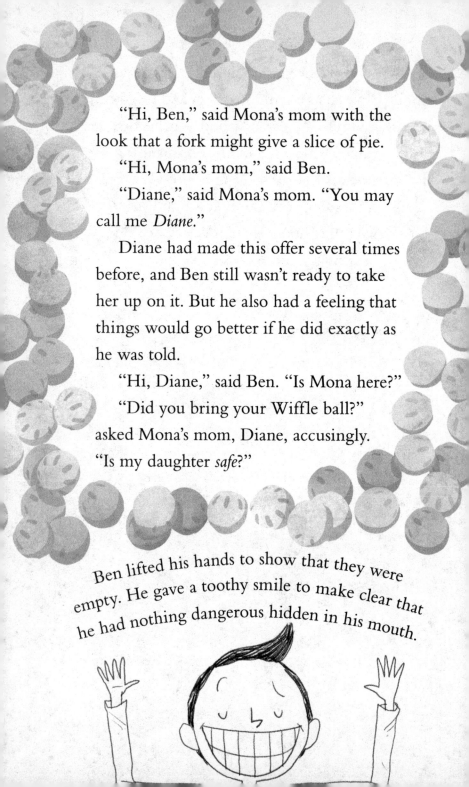

All right, said Mona's mom, Diane, with a face that seemed to say the opposite.

Mona, darling, she called out.

Ben is here.

Mona came out and leaned against the door frame like a soggy old mop leans against a wall. Ben could barely see her eyes beneath the gigantic bandage that covered half her head. Mona's mom, Diane, gave Ben a long, discouraging stare and went inside.

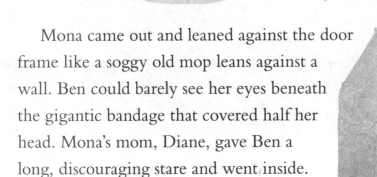

Mona slumped a little and blinked a few times.

Are you here to injure me again?

she asked.

Of course not!

said Ben. He was trying to stay calm but felt a little offended.

Ben had not apologized to that person.

That person was Janet.

They had been playing a kind of tag where instead of tagging with your hand, you tagged by bonking someone with a Wiffle ball. Ben hadn't apologized to Janet because Janet understood that Wiffle balls don't hurt very much, *even when they bonk you in the head!*

Ben thought about pointing this out to Mona, but it seemed like the wrong time.

"I haven't," said Ben. "I'll apologize to her *next,* but I wanted to start by apologizing to *you.* Because you're the one who . . . *suffered.*"

Mona leaned against the door frame again. "Yes, Ben," she said. "And I continue to suffer. Look!" Mona lifted her bandage and pointed to her forehead. There was nothing but a smooth expanse of healthy skin.

Um,

said Ben, wondering what he was supposed to be seeing.

"How does it look, Ben? You can be honest."

"Um," Ben repeated, searching for the words that would allow him to complete his apology and remove himself from Mona's porch as quickly as possible.

"Is it *ghastly*, Ben? My mother says it's ghastly. She says it might not ever heal."

Ben thought about saying,

I have never seen a healthier-looking forehead,

but instead he said,

I'm truly, *truly* sorry.

"I'd *like* to accept your apology," said Mona.

"Great," said Ben, turning to leave.

"But . . . I'd feel better if you could produce a witness who could back up your story."

Ben did not have time for this. Not on his last day.

"I was trying to hit Janet and accidentally hit you," Ben insisted. "I swear!"

"I'd like to hear it from her."

Ben was getting mad. He had done what his mom had asked. It wasn't his fault that Mona wasn't willing to forgive him.

But his mom would know if he didn't actually get Mona to accept his apology.

Drat, darn, and dang! thought Ben, giving Mona the scowl equivalent of a Wiffle ball bonk.

Come with me,

he said, flying off the porch like a Wiffle ball looking for a head to bonk.

Ben hated to bother Janet while she was busy with her latch hook, but he also knew that the sooner he was able to get rid of Mona, the sooner he'd be able to help her with it.

He rang Janet's doorbell.

It took a while, but eventually the door opened. Janet's *Thank goodness you're here* face quickly crumbled into her *Why in the heck did you bring Mona?* face.

"Maybe you can help us with something," said Ben.

Janet looked at her watch. "I'm pretty busy."

"It will only take a second." Ben's eyes said *Please, please, please,* and Janet gave in.

"All right. What is it?"

"Remember the other day when we were playing Wiffle Bonk and I bonked Mona?"

"Sure," said Janet. Ben could tell that she was trying not to smile. "What about it?"

"I was telling Mona that when I accidentally bonked her, I was actually trying to bonk you."

"That's true," said Janet. "One hundred percent."

"Aren't you mad?" Mona asked.

"Nah," said Janet. "It was part of the game. Plus, Wiffle balls don't really hurt."

"They don't?" Mona seemed surprised.

"Not at all," said Janet. "Not if you're tough."

"I'm tough," said Mona, looking less like a mop now and more like a rake.

"Then why are you upset about the accidental bonking?" asked Janet.

"Look!" said Mona, lifting her bandage for Janet.

"Hmm . . . ," said Janet, "I guess you *are* pretty tough."

Mona beamed. "I am."

Ben sensed that they were making progress. "So, do you forgive me?"

"Almost," said Mona, slumping back into a droop.

"Almost?" Ben was losing patience.

"Almost. I definitely forgive Janet for moving out of the way when you threw the ball at her, but I'm not *quite* ready to forgive you for throwing it in the first place."

"Why not?" Ben was exasperated. "It was an *accident!*"

Janet slammed the door, leaving Ben and Mona no closer to a solution.

Ben didn't have time for this! There were still so many things on his list.

But he knew Mona wouldn't be satisfied until she got exactly what she wanted. The question was, *What did Mona want?*

Ben knew how to find out.

You know,

he said, bending over and looking Mona straight in the eye,

this could be *the last day of your life.*

Mona's eyes grew wide, and she opened her mouth to scream.

Ben knew he was walking on a tightrope.

"But . . . it *probably* isn't!"

Mona's mouth closed halfway, but her eyeballs quivered like a bell that just rang and is about to ring again.

"But if it *was*," Ben continued, "*if* it was, what is the thing you'd most want to do on your last day?"

"Hmm," said Mona, distracted by the question and no longer thinking about screaming. *"Hmm."*

She paced back and forth like she was searching for a penny that she'd dropped. Then she stopped and turned to Ben with an excited look.

I'd want to ride your scooter.

Ben was surprised. Ben was delighted. *Could it be that easy?*

"You'd want to ride my scooter?"

"It looks like fun." When Mona smiled, she seemed less miserable. "My mom won't let me try."

Ben pounced.

"*If* I show you how, will you forgive me for bonking you?"

Mona thought about it. "That seems like a fair trade."

Right this way,

said Ben.

He started by riding up and down the block a few times while Mona watched.

That's pretty basic,

said Mona with a bored expression.

Don't you know any tricks?

Ben's neck burned. "Of *course* I know tricks," he said. Which was true. He knew a lot of scooter tricks. It's just that he hadn't quite figured out how to do them. *Yet.*

"I know a really good trick," said Ben, thinking of his list.

Do a perfect tail whip on my scooter

"Let's see it," said Mona.

Ben wasn't sure. A tail whip was tricky. And kind of dangerous. "Maybe later."

"Because it's too hard?"

"It's not hard at all!"

It was the second biggest lie he'd told that week. Every previous attempt to do a tail whip had left Ben lying in an aching heap.

"Then do it!" said Mona.

Ben felt himself making a terrible decision as he scooted slowly to the end of the block. He tried his hardest to make himself stop as he raced back down the sidewalk to build up enough speed. Soon he was going too fast to turn back.

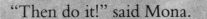

Mona watched him with wide eyes.

Once
Ben got back
to where Mona was
standing, he pulled up
sharply on the handlebars,
which sent the scooter soaring.

Ben landed on
the deck just as the
scooter completed
a full rotation.

It was the perfect tail whip. *Finally.*
Ben felt the joy of a thousand cakes.
Mona erupted in cheers and applause.
Ben got off his scooter and sat in the grass,
feeling like he'd just been elected president.
But he didn't get to celebrate for long.

With his back foot, Ben gave the scooter's tail a quick kick to the left.

Then he whipped the handlebars sharply to the right, which caused the scooter deck to spin around the handle shaft.

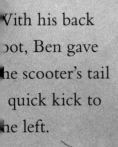

An instant later, the wheels touched back down, and instead of crashing miserably, Ben rolled smoothly down the sidewalk.

My turn!

said Mona.

CHAPTER 17

Ben showed Mona how to stand on the scooter with one foot while pushing with the other.

"Easy as pie," he said, assuming that it must be easier to make a pie than to bake a cake.

"Easy as pie," said Mona, standing on the scooter with one foot while pushing herself along the sidewalk with the other. Ben was surprised at how well she was doing.

Great job! he said.

This is fun,

said Mona, pushing faster.

Ben jogged along beside Mona as she scooted toward the end of the block.

"Wooo!" said Mona, pushing faster and faster. "Wheee!"

"Slow down," said Ben, who was having trouble keeping up.

"How do you do that neat trick?" asked Mona, tugging slightly on the handlebars.

"Don't try the trick!"

"You said it was easy," said Mona. "Were you lying?"

"It's easy if you've practiced a lot," said Ben. "It's not for beginners."

"You said I was doing a great job. Was I, or wasn't I?" asked Mona, going faster and faster.

You *are* doing a great job,

but *don't try the trick!*

But Mona either couldn't hear or didn't want to listen. Ben watched with dismay as she yanked hard on the handlebars and shot up into the air.

At first, Ben was hopeful. It seemed like Mona might just land and keep on rolling down the sidewalk, but the part of her that wanted to do a tail whip collided with the part of her that didn't know how, and the result was a spectacular tumble. Mona went head over heels like a wheel that falls off a wagon and keeps rolling down the road on its own. As she tumbled, she made a sound like a thousand angels crying.

And then she was still. And very quiet.

Ben rushed over and peered down at the aching heap that was Mona. She was starting to catch her breath.

I'm so sorry!

But do you still forgive me?

Mona opened her mouth like she had something to say, but before she could utter a word, her mom screeched in like a runaway ambulance, her eyes like the flashing red lights, her voice like the bellowing siren.

Of *course* she doesn't forgive you! You have injured her *again!*

It's okay if she doesn't forgive me for *this* injury,

said Ben.

This one isn't on my list. I just need to know if she forgives me for the *first* one.

"SHE DOES NOT FORGIVE YOU FOR EITHER ONE,"

screeched Mona's mom, Diane, as she lifted Mona and carried her toward the house. Mona raised her head a little and gave Ben a sly thumbs-up.

He was *pretty* sure this meant that she accepted his apology, that he was forgiven for the bonking, and that he could cross that item off his list.

But Mona's mom,
Diane, wasn't done.

You, Ben Yokoyama, will never ride that scooter again!

You'll never touch another Wiffle ball!

You'll never think another happy thought for the rest of your days!

To prove her wrong,

Ben thought about noodles.

Mona's mom, Diane, went back inside. Ben suspected that she'd eventually tell his parents how he'd tried to murder Mona for the second time.

But as long as she doesn't tell them today, thought Ben, *it might not be a problem at all.*

CHAPTER 18

Ben went back to Janet's and let himself in. She had made good progress on the rug. But there was still a long way to go.

Janet worked on one side and Ben on the other. They were like a beautiful machine.

"What are we doing?" Ben asked.

Janet gave him a look like a question mark gives the rest of the sentence.

"We are making a latch hook rug!"

"I know!" said Ben. "But what is the *verb* for it? Are we *hooking latch*?"

"Hmm . . . ," said Janet.

"Or . . . are we *latching hook*?"

Janet giggled. "Maybe!" she said. "But I'm pretty sure we're just *latch hooking*."

"That sounds right to me," said Ben.

Even when they didn't know the answers, Ben and Janet both liked asking interesting questions.

Ben's friend Kyle didn't care about verbs. Lang wouldn't have been interested, either. Ben liked them both, but this is why Janet was his *best* friend.

Ben suddenly realized why Janet had wanted to make this rug with him on the last day of her life. *Because it was fun. Like baking a cake.* That had been her big idea all along.

"This is fun," said Ben.

"It really is," said Janet with a smile.

He took out his list.

• Make a latch hook rug with Janet

Ben was just about to thank Janet for being wise in a whole new way when she made a sound like a bird smacking into a window.

Oh no, *no*, *no!*

she shrieked, snatching
the rug and holding it up
as if it had suddenly
caught on fire.

What did you *do*, Ben?

Ben was too surprised to speak.
He had no idea what he might have
done to get Janet so upset.

I . . . *latch hooked.* I
thought that's what
we agreed to call it.

Janet's face was a hailstorm.

"*B* is for blue, Ben. Not brown! *BR* is for
brown!"

Janet held up the color key and jabbed at it
with her finger.

And then something clicked, and Ben understood. He had been so focused on the individual pieces of yarn that he'd failed to see the bigger picture.

Instead of being powder blue, Ben's forget-me-nots were earthy brown, as if the petals were dead and dried-up and ready to blow away. It was definitely a mistake. But . . . if the point of making the rug was having *fun* together, Ben wasn't sure why Janet was so upset.

Here.

I can take out the brown. All I have to do is loosen the knots.

At first, Janet looked hopeful. But the knots were too tiny and tight to undo, and she collapsed all over again.

It's ruined!

she wailed.

NO! No! No!

She wasn't even yelling at Ben anymore.
She was just miserable.

Ben had never seen this side of Janet. She
hadn't gotten this upset when Amy Lou
Bonnerman had made fun of her sweater. Or
when she had broken her finger playing soccer.
Not even when her cat had died.

Part of what made Janet *Janet* was that she
kept her cool.

Ben wasn't sure who this new person was.

CHAPTER 19

Janet thundered out of the room and lightninged down the stairs. Ben watched through the window as she went out into the backyard and threw the rug into the black trash can, where they put the leaves.

Then she came back inside and flung herself onto the big blue chair, looking like a sooty, wet, smoldering forest where there's nothing left to burn.

The big blue chair was so big that there was room for Ben to sit there beside her. So he did.

"I'm sorry," said Ben. "I was rushing."

He wanted to say, *I was rushing because there are thousands of squares in that rug and only twenty-four hours in this day.* But he didn't.

You sure were.

Ben didn't want to fight.

"It's just a rug, right?" he said. "Who cares what color those flowers are?"

She'll care!

said Janet with the sharp stab of a bee sting.

And so would *he*!

She burst into tears like a water balloon slamming into a cactus.

Ben didn't know what to do. He wasn't about to say it out loud, and he probably wouldn't even write it in a TOP SECRET DIARY if he had one, but he loved Janet. She was the nonparent person he cared about most. And she was having a really bad day.

Ben pressed his elbow against Janet's elbow, to remind her heart that he was there. Janet pressed her elbow back against Ben's, to let him know that she wasn't done crying yet but was doing her best and appreciated his patience.

They sat there for a while, Janet's sobs growing softer and slower, her breath becoming steadier.

It isn't just a rug,

she said, once she'd calmed down.

It's the rug my dad was making for my mom's birthday but never got to finish before he died.

Oh,

said Ben.

It was the first time Janet had talked about her dad. Ben had never known whether he was dead or just lived somewhere else and never called.

As he settled into knowing the truth, Ben turned sideways in the big blue chair and looked right at Janet. All he wanted to do was make her feel better.

Janet wasn't
looking at Ben.
She was looking
at the lamp.
Or maybe the
wall behind
the lamp.

One morning he was there at breakfast,

she said.

That night Mom and I ate ham sandwiches in the hospital cafeteria.

What happened?

Car accident.

Oh.

Ben got a full-body shiver of sadness. It was just awful. He couldn't imagine living even one day without both of his parents, let alone forever.

Ben's list suddenly got longer, thinking of all the things he wanted to do with his mom and his dad.

He wanted to make it all the way to fifty in Fifty-or-Nothing with his dad. That was for sure. They were stuck on forty-five.

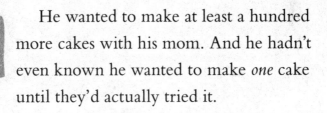

He wanted to make at least a hundred more cakes with his mom. And he hadn't even known he wanted to make *one* cake until they'd actually tried it.

What about all the things he hadn't even thought to put on his list because he didn't yet know that he wanted to do them? The thought gave Ben another full-body shiver.

"I'm pretty sure my dad didn't get a chance to live that day as if it were his last," said Janet. *"Because he didn't know!"*

"How could he?" said Ben, pulling out the fortune and feeling so lucky to have it.

"But you know what?" Janet's eye had just the smallest hint of its old familiar gleam.

"What?" Ben asked, his heart picking itself up just slightly from the floor.

"*I* know how I'm supposed to live this day." Janet looked like herself again. "And so *I* can."

"You sure can," said Ben.

And so I *will*!

Janet stood up. She looked like she was ready to run a race.

"The marshmallows and balloons and stuff weren't my actual list."

"They weren't?"

"Nope. I was just trying to be a good sport because you were so excited about your fortune."

"Thanks," said Ben, who felt a tiny bit tricked.

"But there is something I really have always wanted to do."

"What is it?!" Ben was excited. It was time for the *actual* big thoughts.

"Cut my hair."

Janet's hair was long.

"Why don't you?"

Janet's face got a look like she was taking an extremely tricky math test. But then she swallowed that face and put on a new face like the test was over and she'd gotten a B+.

"There's zero reason not to," she said. "Especially if this is my last day."

"Do it!" said Ben.

"Not me," said Janet.

"What do you mean?"

"You know what I mean."

Ben knew what Janet meant.

And he didn't like it.

CHAPTER 20

Janet picked up a magazine called *Splash*.
She pointed to a picture of a girl whose haircut
looked like the lopsided ring around Saturn.

Janet handed Ben the scissors and gave him a
Come on now, give me a haircut face.

But I don't know how to—

You can do it.

But what if it ends
up looking terrible?

Don't worry.

I don't care.

Even though Janet cared a lot about things that
mattered (like keeping secrets and sticking up for
Ben), she didn't give two hoots about things that
didn't matter at all (like what kind of clothes you
had on or whether you'd ever been to Hawaii).

"I don't know," he said.

"This could be the last day of my life, Ben," said Janet. "I need a haircut, and you're the only one here."

Ben thought about that. She was right. For the first time in his life, he was the best barber in the room.

Janet needed him. He didn't want to let her down again. Plus, giving someone a haircut was another thing he'd never done. Ben had to admit it sounded kind of fun.

He took out his list.

- Make Janet's hair look like the lopsided ring around Saturn

"Hey!" said Janet. But then she took another look at the photo in *Splash*. "You maybe have a point," she admitted.

Ben held the scissors like a pitcher holds a baseball. "Where do I start?"

"Anywhere, I think."

Ben started anywhere. At first, he made tiny, cautious snips, cutting only a few hairs at a time.

But Janet was impatient. "The last day of our lives is racing by!" she insisted. "There's no time for hesitation!"

"Right," said Ben, picking up the pace a little but still going about as quickly as an earthworm runs a marathon.

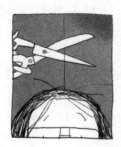

"I *trust* you, Ben," said Janet with the biggest, kindest smile. "Even if this is the worst haircut I get today, it will also be the *best* haircut I get today."

Ben thought about that. It was true.

"Just go for it!" Janet insisted.

Ben decided to go for it. At first, he kept glancing down at the copy of *Splash*, but after a while it became clear that Janet's hair was never going to look like the lopsided ring around Saturn. And so Ben stopped thinking about the picture and just started cutting Janet's hair.

It was the most fun he'd had in a long time, and he was pretty sure Janet felt the same way.

Eventually, Ben stopped. Not because he thought he was done, but because he didn't think Janet would want to be bald.

"Well . . . ?" Ben asked.

"Let me see!" said Janet, racing to the mirror.

Janet looked like a pineapple.
She looked like a planet that had
just been hit by an asteroid.
She looked like a pineapple that
had just been hit by an asteroid.

I love it!

she said, not like she was trying
to make Ben feel good about
himself, but like she actually
meant it.

Janet was looking in the mirror, touching her brand-new short hair, staring into her own eyes like they belonged to a person she wanted to be friends with but didn't quite know how to talk to.

I just *love* it, she said.

She seemed completely satisfied.

But only for a second.

CHAPTER 21

"You know what *else* I've always wanted to do?" Janet was churning again.

"What?"

"Cover my entire face with sticky notes."

Ben loved the idea! It was so *big*!

"Why haven't you done it?"

Janet thought about that. "I'm not sure. I guess it always seemed like a waste of sticky notes."

"But you want to do it now?"

"*Definitely*. I won't be using them tomorrow."

Ben measured Janet's face with his mind.

"How many sticky notes do you have?"

"Plenty. Mom loves her sticky notes."

"What does she use them for?"

"To remember things," said Janet, pointing to the other side of the room.

Ben saw a note
by the door. It said:

"Mom always forgets to bring her umbrella."
Ben noticed another note stuck to the wall by
the doorway that led to the kitchen.

"That one is for me," said
Janet. "I always forget the lights."
"Me too," said Ben.

He suddenly realized that the whole room
was full of sticky notes he'd never noticed
before. They were stuck to the bookcase,
the lamp, and even the TV!

Ben read a few of them.

"What are these for?" asked Ben.

"Mom is constantly thinking up pieces of poems," said Janet. "And she writes them down so she can remember them later."

Ben liked that idea. It made him happy but also sad. He suddenly hoped he would have a lot more days after this one to think up poem pieces and write them down.

Janet handed Ben the pad of sticky notes.

Ben did. It took twenty sticky notes to completely cover her face.

"How do I look?"

To Ben, Janet looked like a person with sticky notes on her face. But he had the sense that Janet wanted more.

"We're almost out of sticky notes," said Ben.

"There are more in the desk drawer."

Ben opened the drawer. There were many pads of sticky notes in many different colors.

"Is pink okay?" asked Ben. He couldn't find more yellow.

"Yes!" said Janet. "Pink is great."

One sticky note at a
time, Ben covered Janet's entire
head. But she still wasn't satisfied.

"Keep going!"

Ben covered Janet's neck and shoulders.
He ran out of pink and had to switch
to green. Then blue. Then purple.

"Keep going!"

Ben covered Janet's arms and legs. And then
the rest of her. Before long, Janet looked like a
great eyeless rainbow-colored bird.

"That's it," said Ben. "I'm done."

The bird spoke. "I need to know what I
look like. You need to take a picture."

"How?" As much as Ben thought he
should have a phone with a camera,
his parents did not agree.

My mom's camera. In
the bottom desk drawer.

Ben found the camera but couldn't make it work. "Hmm . . . ," he said. "The battery is dead."

"Drat!" said Janet.

"I'll go grab my mom's camera," said Ben, suddenly remembering his mom and the cake and his dad and the ice cream and the rest of his life on the other side of the fence.

"Sounds good," said Janet. "But before you go . . ."

"Yes?"

"I'd really like a marshmallow."

Ben grabbed the last bag of marshmallows, lifted the sticky note on Janet's upper lip, and carefully fed her one.

"Thanks," said Janet, "I really needed that. Come back soon, okay?"

"Of course," said Ben, popping a few marshmallows in his pocket for the road. "I absolutely will."

And, at that moment, he absolutely meant it.

153

CHAPTER 22

Ben really didn't feel like riding his scooter all the way around the block. Instead of going out Janet's front door, he went out the back.

There was the fence.

Ben was a very good jumper. He had taken a running leap at the fence a time or two, trying to get his hands high enough to grab the top and pull himself up and over. But he had never been quite tall enough or strong enough. Not *quite*.

Maybe I'm tall enough now, he thought. *Maybe I'm ready today.*

Ben ran toward the fence. He timed his jump perfectly. His fingers touched the top!

But he couldn't manage to hold on, and gravity happened, and he slid down the fence like a meatball slides down the front of your shirt.

Ben lay in an aching heap at the base of the fence. He was glad Janet's eyes were entirely covered with sticky notes.

He stood up, feeling even shorter than he had a moment ago. He hadn't grown enough yet, and he wouldn't by the end of the day.

But instead of letting Ben's body feel sorry for itself, Ben's brain reminded the rest of him that there was something he probably *could* jump over today.

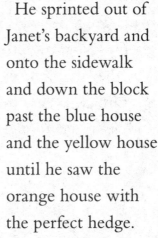

He sprinted out of Janet's backyard and onto the sidewalk and down the block past the blue house and the yellow house until he saw the orange house with the perfect hedge.

Ben crossed his fingers and his heart and hoped that Mr. Hoggenweff would not be in his yard scowling.

Ben looked all around the yard and did not see the keeper of the hedge. He did not see Lovely the grouchy cat. He did not see anything or anyone that could stop him.

He might not have been tall enough to climb over Janet's fence, but he could *absolutely* jump over Mr. Hoggenweff's hedge. He was *almost* entirely sure of it.

Ben veered from the sidewalk and aimed straight for the hedge. To practice, he jumped over a lawn mower. And then over a decorative gnome. Normally, Ben would have wondered why the lawn mower was sitting in the middle of the yard, but there simply wasn't time.

Instead, he thought,

I completed a tail whip on my scooter today. I baked a cake. It wasn't a great cake, but still. I gave someone a haircut. I can do pretty much anything.

The hedge was approaching. It was maybe *slightly* taller than Ben had remembered. On a normal day, he might have turned back. But this day was not normal.

He needed to prove to his legs that they were strong enough and long enough to jump over *something*.

Ben timed the jump *perfectly*. He planted his right foot and shot forward with his left. It was a jump to be proud of. It was exactly the jump you'd want to make on the last day of your life.

But somewhere in the middle of his glorious leap, Ben realized why the yard had been empty.

Mr. Hoggenweff was crouching on the other side of his prizewinning hedge, painting a row of decorative rocks a pleasing shade of blue.

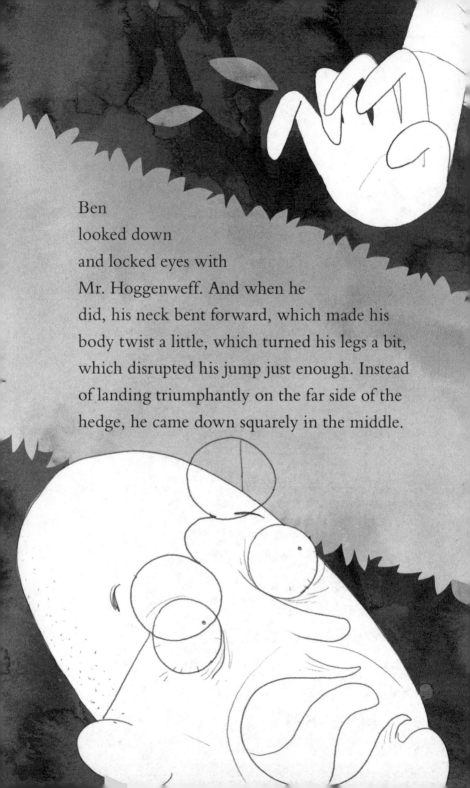

Ben
looked down
and locked eyes with
Mr. Hoggenweff. And when he
did, his neck bent forward, which made his
body twist a little, which turned his legs a bit,
which disrupted his jump just enough. Instead
of landing triumphantly on the far side of the
hedge, he came down squarely in the middle.

Ben
got scratched
and scraped and would
have cried out in pain if he had
not been so completely afraid. His body was
moving so quickly through space that instead of
getting stuck in the hedge, he barreled right
through it.

And because Ben's terrified heart was attached to his panic-stricken legs, instead of stopping to apologize or examine the hedge or see if he was bleeding, he just kept running. Ben heard awful sounds behind him. Shouting and crashing and . . . hissing?

The combination of noises was so interesting that Ben just had to look. As soon as he did, he wished he hadn't.

There was Lovely beside the upside-down paint tray, her previously black fur now a pleasing shade of blue.

There was the hedge, looking like a sheet cake that someone had recently sat on.

And there was Mr. Hoggenweff
with eyes like the end of the world.

Ben *could* have gone back to help out, but it would have been like walking into a burning building, which he knew was not a smart idea, even if you thought it was the right thing to do.

Mr. Hoggenweff was shouting. Ben's anguished ears weren't sure what he was trying to say, but his petrified brain was pretty sure it wasn't *Please come back and have some snickerdoodles.*

Ben kept running. There was no reason to stop. His heart pounded like the bass drum in a rock and roll song.

Maybe the hedge will be fine, thought Ben. Maybe Mr. Hoggenweff hadn't recognized him. Maybe Lovely was ready for a change of hair color.

Maybe, he thought, *they would all sit around and laugh about this someday.*

It was what Ben's dad sometimes said when things seemed awful at the moment but were probably going to be okay in the long run.

Ben thought about his fortune and heaved a deep sigh. There just wasn't time for the long run to matter.

So instead, he made the short run home.

CHAPTER 23

Ben turned onto his own street and glanced at his driveway. The blue car still wasn't there. He glanced at the sky. It was only midafternoon. He glanced at his list. He was doing a pretty good job.

- ~~Jump over Mr. Hoggenweff's prizewinning hedge~~

Ben thought about Janet's list. He couldn't fix the rug, but maybe there was something he *could* do for her, something bigger than getting a camera and taking a picture. Something that would let her know for sure how sorry he was for making the blue flowers brown.

A five-year-old named Patty and a toddler named Eli lived in the house between Ben's and Mrs. Ezra's. They were splashing in a plastic pool in the driveway.

Ben was working on a plan that involved climbing over their fence, but he was going to need their help to pull it off. Or at least their bikes.

"What are you doing?" asked Patty.

"Nothing," said Ben.

"That is not true," said Patty. "You have a sneaky look."

Ben didn't want to get in an argument with Patty, who was just as good as Ben's mom at winning arguments.

I'm going to pick an apple from Mrs. Ezra's yard.

Finally.

What do you mean?

You're always bragging about picking one of her apples, but you never do it.

Ben had to admit that Patty was right. He had more than once mentioned to her how easy it would be to climb over the fence, run across the yard, and pick an apple without being caught by Mrs. Ezra or her dog, Felicity.

"Today I'm actually going to do it."

"I don't believe you."

Ben knew something about Patty.

"Come over here. I have a secret to tell you."

Patty clearly didn't want to do what Ben asked. She put her hands on her hips and refused to be interested. "What?"

Ben didn't want to say it out loud. Eli was too young to hear the grim news. So he leaned in close to Patty's ear and whispered,

This could be the last day of my life.

It isn't.

Maybe not, but it could be.

It's not.

Look, I need to borrow your bike.

No way.

I'll give you a marshmallow.

Let me see it.

Ben reached into his pocket and dug out a marshmallow. It was pretty squished.

It's damaged.

It's still delicious.

Hmm,

said Patty, considering.

One for Eli, too.

Ben reached into his pocket and pulled out the other marshmallow.

"Goo gah," said Eli. To Ben it sounded like, "I don't mind if mine is squished."

"Deal," said Ben, who hated giving up his marshmallows but had a bigger prize in mind.

167

CHAPTER 24

One of the boards in the fence between Mrs. Ezra's yard and Patty's yard had a knothole that was large enough to look through. That was how they knew about the apple tree. That was how they kept an eye on Felicity.

Ben did not feel ready to climb over the fence. "I'm ready," he said.

Patty looked unconvinced.

"Goo gah," said Eli. To Ben it sounded like, "You sure don't look ready."

"I'm ready," said Ben again, trying hard to make it true.

The fence was just as tall as Janet's fence. So Ben stacked Eli's trike on top of Patty's bike to make a kind-of ladder. It was wobbly, but it did the trick.

Ben grabbed the top of the fence with one hand. He pulled himself up and swung one foot over. It was like sitting on a mountain.

There was no sign of Mrs. Ezra. Felicity was sleeping on the back porch.

And there was the tree, full of ripe red apples that were possibly enchanted.

Ben looked back down into Patty's yard.

"The view from here is pretty amazing," he said, watching Patty's face, imagining that she'd be impressed.

Anyone can climb a fence.

Go get that apple.

Her eyes narrowed, and her lips snarled a little. Ben wondered how a five-year-old could be so menacing.

Goo gah, said Eli. To Ben it sounded like, "You haven't accomplished anything yet."

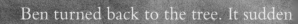

Ben turned back to the tree. It sudden

I don't believe in witch
But I really don't want

Janet doesn't need this apple was th
Plus, this might . . . not . . . be the last d
There could be plenty of time to pick he

Ben was just about to climb bac
dad, who would never be able t

:emed very far away.

:hought Ben.
nd out the hard way that I'm wrong, he thought next.

ext thought that came into his head.
my life . . . or Janet's.
n enchanted apple some other *day.*

own into Patty's yard when he thought of Janet's
inish making the rug or pick an apple for Janet.

But Ben *could*. And so he had to try.

171

CHAPTER 25

Ben let himself down into Mrs. Ezra's yard and realized with a gulp that he didn't have any kind of ladder to climb back out.

He was stuck. But he would worry about that later. For now, he had an apple to pick.

Goo gah, said Eli through the knothole. To Ben it sounded like, "Mrs. Ezra could be casting witch spells on you at this very moment."

Ben looked up at Mrs. Ezra's house. He had never realized how many windows it had. *Eleven!* There were *eleven* windows on the back of the house, and Mrs. Ezra could be looking through any one of them.

Ben glanced down at his hands to see if he had grown troll fingers, but they still seemed like kid fingers for the moment.

Yawn, Patty said, instead of actually yawning.

Goo gah, said Eli, which sounded to Ben like, "This is more boring than that show with the two dancing flowers."

Ben knew what had to be done. Janet needed him. There was no time to be afraid.

He walked toward the tree until he reached the base of the trunk. Then he placed his foot and jumped, grabbing the lowest branch and pulling himself up.

Suddenly he was surrounded by hundreds of bright red apples. *Everything was going so well!* Ben reached out and picked the most beautiful apple he had ever seen. He didn't know whether it was enchanted, but it sure looked delicious. He couldn't wait to give it to Janet.

Ben looked over at Patty and held up the apple in triumph.

But instead of cheering or giving him the thumbs-up or otherwise telling Ben how brave and impressive he was, she was pointing toward Mrs. Ezra's back porch.

Felicity began to bark.
For a small dog, she made a
big sound, like a chain saw
starting or a whale trying on
an uncomfortable raincoat.

Felicity was over near the hole in the fence,
barking at Patty. But Patty was pointing at
something else now. She was pointing toward . . .
the tree.

That's when Ben noticed Mrs. Ezra
standing beside the tree, glaring
right up at him with eyes
that burned like the
coils inside an oven.

*How had she walked across
the yard without him noticing?!*

Deep in his heart, Ben
knew.

It was just the sort of thing
that witches did.

CHAPTER 26

 said Ben.

I'll get out of your
yard right away!

He closed his eyes, wondering if he
would still enjoy the taste of noodles as a troll.

You won't come down, and
you won't get out of my yard.

Mrs. Ezra's voice was fierce and certain.
It wasn't what Ben had expected to hear.
He opened his eyes. Mrs. Ezra's expression
was impossible to understand. He wished
his mom were there to tell him what
to call it.

I *won't?*

You certainly will not.

What *am* I going to do? Ben wondered if he would spend the rest of his last day in an apple tree.

"You're going to pick a basket of apples for me," said Mrs. Ezra, handing a basket up to Ben.

"All right," said Ben, taking the basket and wondering if this was like the part in "Hansel and Gretel" where the witch fattened up the children to make them more delicious.

"And . . . you're going to tell me a story while you pick them."

"I *am*?"

"You *are*. You know the one I want to hear."

"I *do*?"

"You certainly do."

Mrs. Ezra sat down on a lawn chair near the tree and put on her sunglasses. She was wearing a hat that belonged on the head of a queen from a different century. Or maybe an extremely fancy witch.

Ben had no idea what she was talking about. But since she hadn't turned him into a troll—so far—he decided to do whatever he could to keep her happy.

While Ben picked apples and placed them in the basket, he searched the deepest corners of his memory for something Mrs. Ezra might like to hear. But his heart was pounding, and his mind was racing, and just one story came to mind.

There was this boy, and it was the last day of his life.

Is this a sad story?

Mrs. Ezra looked up at Ben,
but because of the sunglasses,
he couldn't see her eyeballs.

It might be, said Ben, picking an apple
and placing it the basket.

I'm not sure yet.

I don't much care for sad
stories, but keep going.

Ben kept going.

The boy helped his
mom bake a cake.

Mrs. Ezra took off her sunglasses
and looked straight at Ben as if he
had said something shocking.

What kind of cake?

It was supposed to be a blueberry-
lemon buttermilk chiffon cake with
Italian buttercream frosting.

"What do you mean, 'supposed to be'? What happened to it?"

"Something went wrong."

"This story just got interesting." Mrs. Ezra nodded at Ben and put her sunglasses back on. "Life is full of disappointing cakes, but we get out fresh ingredients and try again, don't we?"

"Or else we buy one at Far Alfredo's," said Ben, glancing over to his driveway to see if the blue car was back. It wasn't.

Mrs. Ezra snorted, and Ben wasn't sure if he'd said the right thing.

She gave him a stern look. "Is that the end of the story?"

"No," said Ben. "Next, the boy gave his best friend a haircut. And he jumped over a really high hedge. And he taught a little girl how to ride a scooter."

"That's all very interesting," said Mrs. Ezra, "but it feels like you must have skipped something."

"What do you mean?" asked Ben, who knew exactly what.

"Usually along with all the good things that happen in a story, there are parts that are bumpy. Doesn't your story have any bumps?"

Ben picked an apple and thought about the bumps. There were so many to choose from.

"The boy ate something he wasn't supposed to."

"And?"

"He spilled some paint on a grouchy cat."

"And . . . ?"

"He messed up someone's extremely special latch hook rug."

Mrs. Ezra took off her sunglasses and looked straight into Ben's soul. "It's a *much* better story now, don't you think?"

"Yes," said Ben, hoping his story was now bumpy enough that she would let him go back home.

"But the story isn't finished," said Mrs. Ezra. "Shall we see how it ends?"

"Okay," said Ben, who wasn't sure at all.

"The next thing that happens is that the boy climbs down from the tree and carries the apples inside."

Mrs. Ezra stood under the tree and reached up toward Ben.

And here comes the part where she throws me into the oven, he thought.

But then Ben realized Mrs. Ezra was just reaching for the basket. He handed it down to her.

"This should be plenty," she said, taking the basket of apples and setting it at the base of the tree. "Come along, then."

Mrs. Ezra whistled to Felicity, who scampered in circles near her feet as she walked back toward the house.

Ben climbed down from the tree and looked over at the fence, wishing for a ladder or an oak tree.

"Goo gah," said Eli, but to Ben it sounded like, "It was nice knowing you, Ben. Can I have your scooter?"

Ben gave a weary smile and a final wave as he picked up the basket of apples and followed Mrs. Ezra around her house, through the side door, and into an uncertain fate.

CHAPTER 27

Ben put the apples on Mrs. Ezra's kitchen counter. Her house smelled like Halloween spices. He looked around for a black cat or broomsticks or troll children, but everything seemed perfectly ordinary.

Still, he didn't want to take any chances. "Sorry, but I have to go home now," he said. "My mom is expecting me."

"We're not quite done," said Mrs. Ezra in a cold, flat voice that made clear going home was not an option.

She opened a drawer and pulled out two small but wicked-looking knives. Ben was sad and afraid and got goose bumps with goose bumps on top. His fortune had been right. He was thankful that the other parts of his last day had been so good.

But then Mrs. Ezra handed one of the knives to Ben. "These apples aren't going to peel themselves," she said.

Ben felt relieved and then guilty for jumping to conclusions.

He had always used a peeler to peel apples and carrots and potatoes, but the knife worked just as well.

They peeled and peeled those apples.

Why did you climb over my fence?

Mrs. Ezra gave Ben a scowl like a trout gives a fishing hook.

Ben paused. The answer was complicated. He thought of a million excuses but decided to tell the truth instead.

"Because my
friend was sad, and
I thought having one
of your apples would
make her feel better."

"Why didn't you just ask
me for one?"

"Because . . ." Ben decided
not to tell the truth this time.

Mrs. Ezra gazed deep into his eyes.

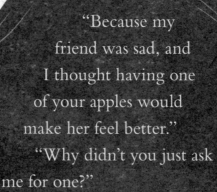

Because you think
I'm a witch?

"Of course not!" said Ben. "Witches are
imaginary," he added, as if trying to convince
both of them.

"That's ridiculous," said Mrs. Ezra, looking at
Ben like a match looks at a candlewick.

I am a witch!

"You are?"

"Of course I am. Look," she said, pointing to a fat orange cat asleep on the windowsill. "That's Roger. He's extremely fierce."

"But . . ." Ben was confused. "Aren't witch cats supposed to be black?"

Instead of answering his question, Mrs. Ezra asked one of her own.

"Why does your friend want my apples so badly?"

Ben said what he thought to be true.

"She thinks they're . . . enchanted . . . and wants to know what magic tastes like. She's wanted to know for a really long time."

"I like the sound of this girl. What made you decide to come get it . . . this afternoon?"

"Well," said Ben, leaning in little, "this could be the last day of our lives."

"That's absolutely true," said Mrs. Ezra, without looking up from her peeling.

Ben was surprised. Pretty much everyone had been trying to talk him out of believing his fortune. And now that someone actually agreed with it, he kind of wished she didn't. Ben looked sadly out the window. The sun would soon set. There wasn't much of his last day left.

"I'm glad you understand," he said.

"Certainly, I do," said Mrs. Ezra. "It could be the last day of my life as well."

"Because you're so old?" Ben asked before realizing it was probably a rude thing to say.

"I'm not old at all," said Mrs. Ezra, but she didn't seem offended. "Yet it could be my last day just the same. Which is why I try to live every day *as if* it were my last."

"Because you read it in a fortune cookie?"

"No. Because it helps me remember to spend *every* day doing the things that are most important to me."

Ben looked at Mrs. Ezra and wondered if she was the kind of person who had big thoughts, too. He decided to find out.

"What would you want to do if this *were* your last day?"

Mrs. Ezra put down her knife and gave Ben a smile. It turned her face into something entirely new.

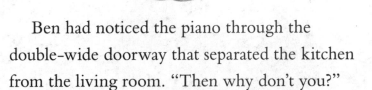

I would want to play the Sonata in D Major by Mozart, of course.

Ben had noticed the piano through the double-wide doorway that separated the kitchen from the living room. "Then why don't you?"

"It's a duet. Which requires four hands. I only have two."

She held them up for Ben to see. They were wrinkled but seemingly strong.

Ben was suddenly glad about his piano lessons. "I also have two."

"I had noticed that," said Mrs. Ezra with a smile. She led Ben into the living room and gestured to the piano bench. He sat down, and Mrs. Ezra squeezed in beside him. There was plenty of room for both of them.

Mrs. Ezra already knew her part, and Ben read his from the sheet music. He went kind of slow and made a few mistakes, but it sounded pretty good.

How was that?

he asked.

Mrs. Ezra didn't say a word. Her smile did all the talking.

Out the window, Ben saw
the blue car pulling back into
the driveway.

"That's my mom," said Ben.

"You'd better go," said Mrs.
Ezra. "Will you let me borrow
your two hands again
sometime?"

"I definitely will," said Ben.
"Unless this is . . . you know."

"Yes," said Mrs. Ezra. *"Unless."*

Ben was halfway out the door when she said,
"Wait just a minute. I think you're forgetting
something."

He turned to look and broke into the biggest
smile.

Mrs. Ezra was holding the ripest, reddest,
most enchanted-looking apple Ben had ever seen.

CHAPTER 28

All Ben wanted to do was take the apple to Janet,
but first he had to check on the cake situation.
When he got back inside, his mom was taking
the clear plastic lid off the cake she had
bought at Far Alfredo's.

What do you think? Does it
look like the cake you ate?

Ben took a close look. It *sort of*
did. It was the *shape* of a cake.
The frosting was light yellow,
which was the right color, at least.

I think so. Or pretty close.

Great. Now all we have to do is cut a piece
and put a few blueberries on top, wrap it
in plastic, and put it in the freezer.

Ben put the apple on the counter and got out
the special knife they used to cut cake.
He handed the knife to his mom.

"Here goes," she said.

"We did it," said Ben.

She cut into the cake.

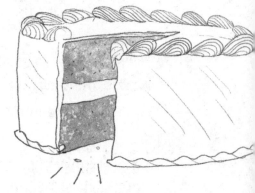

The insides were
bright orange.

First, Ben's mom made a sound that wasn't a
word and a face that no words could have ever
described. And then she said, "*Orange!* Who
makes the inside of a cake *orange,* Ben? *Who?*"

Ben was pretty sure his mom wasn't asking an
actual question, so he decided not to give her an
actual answer.

Then she slumped against
the counter and started to
cry. It wasn't a thing she
did very often.

Ben had to do something, so he did.

"I'll be right back," he said.

Ben walked down the block and knocked on Mrs. Ezra's door.

Hello again!

she said with shining eyes.

Excuse me,

said Ben, getting right to the point.

But do you know how to make a blueberry-lemon buttermilk chiffon cake with Italian buttercream frosting?

A few minutes later, Ben was back at his house. His mom was vacuuming the living room again. He knew they had to get rid of the cake with orange insides before his dad saw it.

Ben looked at Dumbles, who was sleeping in the corner, and briefly considered asking for his help. But Ben knew some challenges were meant to be faced on one's own.

Ben took out his list. He knew what had to be done.

· Eat a whole cake at once

Ben ate that cake like a tornado eats a field of summer corn. When he was finished, not a single crumb of evidence remained.

Holding his stomach and groaning a little, Ben told his mom the rest of the plan.

She looked hopeful but worried. "Do we have enough time?"

Ben looked at the clock and did some math. "*Just* enough time."

"Whew," said Ben's mom. "Thank you, Ben!"

"Thank Mrs. Ezra."

They played a few more games of *Whoops!*, but Ben's mom kept looking at the clock and forgetting to say *Whoops!*, so Ben won every time.

Whoops!

said Ben.

Oh man,

said his mom, shaking her head. She wasn't used to losing at anything, but for the moment, at least, she was too distracted to care.

Ha, ha, ha,

said Ben, taking all the cards so he could shuffle them again.

They heard a sound in the driveway. It was the green car. About a half hour too soon.

"Dad must have driven really, really fast," said Ben.

"Whoops!" said his mom, looking panicked again.

"Everything is going to be all right," said Ben, who actually believed it.

"Is it?" asked his mom, who didn't look like she believed it at all.

"It is," said Ben. "We just need to stall him a little bit longer."

Ben's mom forced a smile.

Watch the master,

she said.

CHAPTER 29

Ben's dad burst in with a smile that looked like the St. Louis Arch would look if the St. Louis Arch were a whole lot smaller and also upside down.

"You got it?" asked Ben's mom.

"I got it!" said Ben's dad, handing her a container of ice cream.

"My hero!" said Ben's mom, grabbing a spoon and taking two huge bites. "*Oh my goodness,* it's delicious." She clearly wasn't faking this part.

Ben's dad looked as happy as a seal on a bright sunny rock.

It's almost time for your big surprise! Nora will be here soon to watch Ben while we . . .

But instead of finishing that sentence, Ben's dad started another.

How about you go put on whatever you were wearing exactly . . . nine years, three months, and seventeen days ago?

Ben's mom did some math.

You mean my wedding dress?

That's the one!

I'm pretty sure I don't fit into it anymore.

How about a different dress, then? We should probably leave in about twenty minutes.

Ben's mom gave Ben a look that meant, *That's not enough time, is it?*

Ben gave her a look that meant, *It's definitely not. Can you talk about dresses some more?*

Ben's mom turned back to Ben's dad. "It might be that . . . *all* of my dresses are dirty."

"*All* of them?"

"It's possible."

"But I'm pretty sure you have some pants."

"I . . . *do* have some pants."

"Well, I don't care at all what you wear. Just be ready to go in twenty minutes!" Ben's dad was glowing like a street full of neon signs at night.

Ben could tell his mom had run out of excuses. It was his turn.

Exciting news, Dad!

What is it? Ben's dad was a sucker for exciting news.

Right this way,

said Ben, leading his dad away from the kitchen and hoping that something both exciting and newsworthy would suddenly happen in the living room.

But there had never been a less newsworthy room in the history of rooms.

Ben and his dad stood there blinking at each other.

"Well?" said Ben's dad, eagerly awaiting the excitement.

"Well . . . ," said Ben. "You see . . ."

The problem was, Ben *didn't* see.

Oh!

said Ben's dad.

Oh?

asked Ben.

Wow!

his dad said.

You did it. You put together the Taj Mahal!

Yes! I did,

said Ben.

I sure did. *That's* the exciting thing I wanted to show you.

Ben's dad spent a long time looking at every last detail of the Taj Mahal. He opened the openable door and removed the removable dome and admired the strip of shiny plastic that was supposed to look like a reflecting pool. But it still took only a few minutes.

Well, that was about as much excitement as I can handle,

said Ben's dad, glancing sideways at his watch when he thought Ben wasn't looking.

I'd better go see how your mom is doing.

The doorbell rang.

I'll get it,

said Ben's dad, who loved answering the door as much as a bee loves being jammed into a hive with ten thousand other bees.

It's probably Nora.

But Ben knew that Nora was always late. The person at the door had to be Mrs. Ezra with the replacement cake.

Ben's dad was just about to open the door when Ben's mom rushed in with a look of pure panic. She also knew that Nora was always late.

I'll answer the door,

she insisted.

And you . . . go get dressed for our big evening.

"I'm already dressed!" said Ben's dad.

It was true. He was already wearing his stylish pink shirt.

"Right," said Ben's mom, giving Ben her *What do we do now?* face and trying to figure out another good reason why Ben's dad definitely shouldn't answer the door.

Owwww!

Ben howled, clutching his right foot and hopping wildly away from the front door and back toward the living room.

Ben's dad was concerned. "Linda! Something is wrong with Ben!"

"This looks like something *only you* can handle!" she insisted.

"It does?" Ben's dad didn't seem sure. Ben's mom was the one who usually took care of things when Ben was sick or hurt.

"Absolutely," she said. "I'd *never* know how to help him with . . . *this particular problem*. I'll answer the door, and you go help Ben like *only you can.*"

"All right," said Ben's dad, sounding capable and proud. "I'll do it."

Ben's dad rushed into the living room, where Ben was still hopping up and down and holding his foot as if it were on fire. "What seems to be the problem, Ben?"

OW!

Ben tried his hardest to drown out the sound of
Mrs. Ezra explaining that it wasn't the *very* best
cake she'd ever made because she'd had to hurry,
and it probably should have cooled a bit longer,
but that she hoped it would do the trick.

Who is it?

shouted Ben's dad,
who simply couldn't
stand to not know.

Vacuum saleswoman!
There's a new kind,
apparently,

Ben's mom shouted.

Ben's dad's eyes lit up like a suburban cul-de-sac in December. "You know, I've been thinking we could use a new vacuum." He started to walk toward the door.

"*Owwwwwwwww!*" Ben moaned, falling to the floor and clutching his belly.

Aaaaaaaaahhhhhh!

"*Ben!*" said his dad, bending over Ben to see what was wrong.

Ben heard the front door close. He watched over his dad's shoulder as his mom tiptoed through the living room with the cake and disappeared into the kitchen. *The plan was working!*

But now she needed to cut a piece and wrap it in plastic and freeze it at least a little and hide the rest of the cake somewhere that Ben's dad wouldn't find it.

I have an idea about where to hide the rest of that cake, thought Ben.

His mom popped her head in from the kitchen with her *Can you please try to get your dad a bit farther away from the kitchen?* face.

Ben gave her a wink that meant, *This plan is getting extremely complicated, but I will do my best.*

Ben stood up. "I suddenly feel much better," he said. And before his dad could say *Wow* or *Gosh, what a speedy recovery* or *Is it just me, or is something fishy going on?,* Ben turned and pointed out the window and said, "Holy smokes, would you look at that!" And then he walked confidently through the back door.

Ben crossed his fingers and toes, hoping against hope that his dad would follow.

Luckily, he did.

CHAPTER 30

There they were in the backyard.

"What did you want me to see, Ben?"
His dad sounded sort of maybe almost halfway
frustrated.

Ben glanced around desperately for something
worth seeing. But there was nothing except . . .

"The wheelbarrow!" he said, noticing the
upside-down wheelbarrow near the pile of mulch
that had never been spread.

Ben's dad looked at the
wheelbarrow. "What about it?"

"Does it seem strange to you?"

"What do you mean?" His dad
walked over to the wheelbarrow and
turned it right side up.

Seems fine to me.

"Whew," said Ben, as if someone had just prevented a clumsy kitten from falling into a swimming pool.

"What's going on, Ben?" His dad was definitely starting to get suspicious.

Just then Ben saw something that made his heart leap.

"Look!" he said. And this time he meant it.

"Ben!" said his dad, who was getting a little fed up with being told to look.

"No, really. *Look!*" said Ben, pointing at the ground.

The wheelbarrow had been upside down for a long time, which is why Ben hadn't been able to find the baseball mitts for a long time, but there they were, right in the middle of the patch of dead grass where the upside-down wheelbarrow had been.

Ben had put the mitts under the wheelbarrow to keep them dry one day when it had started to rain, and he'd been searching for them ever since.

"Want to play catch?" Ben asked his dad.

Ben's dad glanced at his watch.

"Fifty-or-Nothing!" said Ben.

It was a game where they started by standing close together and then threw the ball back and forth. Each time they caught it, they counted and took a step back, and the point was to get all the way to fifty without dropping the ball.

They had never gotten all the way to fifty without dropping the ball.

"We have to try," said Ben. "Because it could be . . ."

"The last day of our lives," said his dad, nodding in agreement. "We *definitely* do."

Ben needed to make sure his dad was facing *away* from the house so that there was no chance he would see what Ben's mom was up to in the kitchen.

Just for fun, how about you face the yard, and I'll face the house?

Ben suggested, hoping his dad would go along with it.

"But you always face the yard." His dad looked puzzled but also pleased. *"Always."*

"That's true," said Ben. He preferred to face the yard because the oak tree kept the afternoon sun out of his eyes.

"But on the last day of my life, I want to see what the yard looks like from over where you're standing."

Ben's dad smiled. "I completely understand. All day I've been wearing my watch on my left wrist instead of my right."

211

"Why?"

"Just to see how it feels."

"How does it feel?"

"*Different.* Sometimes different is good. Often it is."

Ben thought about that. So much about today had been different. So much about today had been good.

They put on their mitts and stood toe-to-toe. "One," said Ben. He tossed the ball a few inches and took a small step back.

"Two," said his dad, tossing the ball and taking a step back himself.

"Three," said Ben. He had forgotten all about stalling to give his mom time. He was just happy to have found the mitts. Happy to be playing catch with his dad.

"Four," said his dad.

"Five!" said Ben.

They went back and forth like that as the sun dropped lower in the sky.

"Forty-five," said Ben a few minutes later.

Their record was forty-five. They had never made it to forty-six.

"This is it," said Ben's dad. "The moment we've been waiting for."

"We can do it," said Ben.

"We must."

Ben threw the ball, and his dad caught it.

"Forty-six!" Ben shouted. "New record! Should we quit while we're ahead?"

"Fifty or nothing," his dad said, taking a step back.

"Fifty or nothing," said Ben.

Ben's dad threw the ball.

"Forty-seven," said Ben as he caught it. He took a step back.

"Forty-eight," said his dad, taking a step back.

"Forty-nine," said Ben, taking a huge step back.

His dad was all the way across the yard. It was going to take all of Ben's strength to throw that far. He threw with all his might and let the ball fly.

But somehow, he threw it *too* far. His dad tried to catch it, but it sailed over his head and bounced against the side of the house.

"Oh no!" said Ben's dad, laughing. "Shall we try again?"

Ben's mom poked her head through the kitchen window and gave Ben a thumbs-up.

Part of him wanted to try again. Part of him wanted to keep on throwing the ball forever so the day would never end. But the other part knew that his dad had a special dinner planned and that he had been very patient already.

And . . . Ben remembered . . . he still owed Janet an apple. *And a camera!* As soon as his parents left for their date, he would climb over the fence and take them to her.

Not today,

said Ben.

Hopefully . . . tomorrow?

Hopefully, tomorrow,

his dad said, giving Ben a great big sideways hug as they walked back toward the house.

Hopefully.

When they got back inside, the doorbell was ringing. And ringing. Whoever it was must have had something pretty important to say.

CHAPTER 31

The doorbell rang again. And again.

"Who could it be?" asked Ben's dad.

"It's probably Nora," said Ben's mom.

Ben hoped it was Nora, but based on the endless angry ringing, he feared that it probably wasn't.

Ben's parents were walking toward the door. He scampered and got there first.

Wait, he said.

Wait.

The day was going so well. He wasn't ready for everything to fall apart.

Wait for what? asked his dad.

What's going on? asked his mom.

Well…, said Ben.

There were so many things he could have said. But none of them were going to stop the door from opening eventually. "Maybe you should just open it," said Ben, who knew that sometimes it was better to get right to the point.

Ben's mom looked at his dad, and his dad looked at his mom. Ben looked at Dumbles, who was patiently waiting to sniff the shoes of whoever it happened to be.

Ben's mom opened the door. There was Mr. Hoggenweff. And there was Mona's mom, Diane.

Mr. Hoggenweff was holding Lovely, who was still mostly blue. Mona's mom, Diane, was holding Mona, whose entire head was wrapped in bandages, with just a narrow slit for Mona to see through.

Everyone was frowning, especially Lovely. It was hard to know if Mona was frowning, because Ben couldn't see her mouth.

"Hello," said Ben's mom. There was nothing else to say.

Mr. Hoggenweff and Mona's mom, Diane, looked as mad as two clams being forced to live inside the same shell. They seemed as angry at each other as they were at Ben as they stood there wrestling with their elbows to see who would get to complain first.

Mr. Hoggenweff didn't wait to find out.

Lovely is blue! And my prizewinning hedge is *dented.*

Before Ben's parents could respond, Mona's mom, Diane, took her turn.

Ben placed Mona's life in terrible danger! She may never recover!

Ben's parents stood there like they were watching a movie about explosions.

They looked at Lovely and they looked at Mona's head. They looked at each other. They looked at Ben.

"What?" said Ben. Ben knew what.

"Well?" said Mr. Hoggenweff, holding up Lovely.

"Well?" said Mona's mom, Diane, nodding at Mona's bandaged head.

"Ben?" said Ben's mom.

Ben suddenly forgot how to speak the English language.

"Excuse me," said someone. Everyone turned to see who the voice belonged to. It was Mrs. Ezra, who was suddenly standing there, calm as a puddle on a day with no wind. "I hope I'm not interrupting," she said, "but I heard some commotion over here and thought I'd come by and see if I could help."

"We don't need help!" wailed Mona's mom, Diane. "We need *justice*!"

Oh, you poor dear,

said Mrs. Ezra, looking at the mummy-headed mess that was Mona.

"Excuse me," said Mr. Hoggenweff, as prickly as an irritated porcupine, "but what about Lovely? She is—"

"You will wait your turn, young man," said Mrs. Ezra, cutting him off with the look that a set of garden shears might give to an overgrown hedge.

Ben's mom swallowed a snort and managed to stifle her laugh. Mr. Hoggenweff's eyes bulged with rage, and his cheeks turned pink. He looked like someone who needed to sneeze but couldn't quite get there. To the amazement of everyone, he kept quiet while Mrs. Ezra continued.

"Where were we?" she said, turning back to Mona and her mom.

"My daughter has been badly injured!"

"What happened . . . exactly?"

"She fell off a scooter."

"How did she get *on* the scooter?"

This . . . *monster* . . . forced her to ride it.

I didn't! Ben protested.

You must have, said Mona's mom, Diane.

He didn't! came a voice from under the bandages.

At least that's what it sounded like. The voice was rather muffled.

"What was that?" asked Mrs. Ezra. "Louder, please."

"Don't say a word, darling," said Mona's mom, Diane. "Just *rest*."

But Mona didn't listen.

And even though Ben couldn't see mummy Mona's mouth, he could tell she was smiling.

"She must have a fever!" said Mona's mom, Diane. "She's *delirious!*"

"I entirely agree," said Mrs. Ezra.

"You *do?*" said Mona's mom, Diane.

"You *do?*" said both of Ben's parents at the very same time.

"Oh yes," said Mrs. Ezra. "Which means Mona's injuries must be quite *serious.*"

"They are!" said Mona's mom, Diane. "I might even call them *dire!*"

"In which case, I think it's extremely important that Ben take a good hard look at them," said Mrs. Ezra, "so that he can learn the consequences of his recklessness."

"But her head is covered in bandages," said Ben.

"Exactly," said Mrs. Ezra, "which is why we'll have to take them off."

"We *can't!*" gasped Mona's mom, Diane. "We *won't!*"

"*I* can!" said Mona with delight. "*I* will!" She wriggled out of her mother's arms and stood on the porch.

My legs aren't broken! I'm *well* again!

Mona started unwrapping her bandages like a hungry parrot unwraps a pack of crackers.

"No, darling!" Mona's mom, Diane, used one frantic arm to halfway pick Mona back up and the other to try to hold the bandages in place.

But it was no use. Mona was surprisingly determined. And extremely wriggly. A moment later, she stood there with all her bandages removed. And . . . not a single scrape or bruise on her face.

"She's healed!" Mrs. Ezra declared. "It's a miracle!"

"Hooray!" said Mona, leaping off the porch and running down the sidewalk toward her house.

"My darling!" screamed Mona's mom, Diane, lunging after Mona.

Slow down!

Come back!

Wait for me!

Ben's mom and dad looked like they were watching a movie about a flock of disturbed geese.

What a wonderful family,

said Mrs. Ezra
with a satisfied sigh.

CHAPTER 32

Mr. Hoggenweff cleared his throat.

You're still here?

asked Mrs. Ezra, squinting at him like a librarian squints at an overdue book.

Mr. Hoggenweff was still there. He seemed pleased to have the porch to himself. "I am not leaving this porch until *justice has been served!*"

"Of course!" said Mrs. Ezra. "And you shall have it!"

Ben was trying to figure out whose side she was on.

"I certainly hope so," said Mr. Hoggenweff, who seemed to be wondering the same thing.

Mrs. Ezra looked Ben straight in the eyes. "Are you sorry, Ben?"

"Very, very sorry," said Ben. And he meant it. He felt terrible about the hedge *and* about Lovely.

"Well?" said Mrs.
Ezra to Mr. Hoggenweff.
"Sometimes sorry is not enough!"
he said like a puffer fish making
itself completely round and pointy.
"What do you want . . . exactly?"
asked Ben's mom.

I want Ben to water my hedge.

"Well, that seems reasonable," said
Ben's dad. "Don't you
think so, Ben?"

Ben did not want to water the hedge because
he didn't want to be within one hundred feet of
Mr. Hoggenweff. But he had to admit that it
seemed reasonable. After all, he had damaged the
hedge. And Lovely *was* blue. It made
sense for him to set things right.

It does, said Ben, nodding.

"How often would you like Ben to water the hedge?" asked Mrs. Ezra.

"Every day, of course!" Mr. Hoggenweff replied, as if offended by the question.

"For how long? Maybe a week. Or even two?"

Mr. Hoggenweff's eyes grew wide with indignation. "*A week?!* I was thinking *at least* six months. Or a full year!" Mr. Hoggenweff looked very proud of himself.

Six months? said Ben.

Or a full year? said Ben's mom and Ben's dad at the very same time.

Yes, that seems entirely reasonable.

It does? said Ben, who didn't think it sounded reasonable at all.

Yes, it certainly does. But . . . .

Mrs. Ezra paused, as if she had remembered something extremely important.

"Yes?" said Mr. Hoggenweff.

"I really shouldn't say."

But Mr. Hoggenweff was extremely curious. "You should say. You *must*."

"Well," said Mrs. Ezra in the most serious of voices, "this family is too polite to tell you, but this could be the last day of Ben's life."

What do you mean? What's wrong with him?

"I'm afraid that's . . . private," said Mrs. Ezra as mysteriously as possible.

Ben caught on. He coughed a little. His parents looked like they were watching a movie about a bowling ball balanced on top of a broomstick.

That's . . . terrible, said Mr. Hoggenweff, stepping back a little and covering Lovely's mouth with his hand.

Is it . . . contagious?

"Hopefully not," said Mrs. Ezra. "But . . . you never know."

Now Mr. Hoggenweff was backing very carefully down the porch steps.

"You have to go already?" asked Mrs. Ezra. "That's too bad. What time would you like Ben to come tomorrow?"

"Tomorrow?" Mr. Hoggenweff's scowling eyes had been replaced by worried ones.

"To water the dent in your prizewinning hedge. What time should he be there?"

"That's quite all right. I should be able to handle the watering on my own."

"Well, all right," said Mrs. Ezra. "If you say so."

Once Mr. Hoggenweff reached the bottom of the steps, he started to walk rather quickly. When he reached the edge of the yard, he broke into a full scurry.

Ben watched as Mr. Hoggenweff scampered down the street and around the corner. His parents looked like they were watching a movie about a daring heist that succeeds against all odds.

It was very quiet on the porch. That's when they realized that Mrs. Ezra was holding an apple pie.

I hear we have an anniversary to celebrate,

she said.

CHAPTER 33

They invited Mrs. Ezra in to join them for pie, which they served with generous scoops of double fudge banana frost ice cream.

Having dessert before dinner was one of Ben's favorite things, *even if* the dinner was noodles.

Everyone was in a glorious mood. They all felt as if they had accomplished something important.

"I hope you will continue to pick apples for me, Ben," said Mrs. Ezra, who was quickly becoming one of Ben's favorite people.

I will,

said Ben, but because his mouth was so full, it sounded instead like the half-hearted howl of an extremely sleepy wolf.

"Manners, Ben," said Ben's mom, who occasionally tried to say the sorts of things that moms were supposed to say, even if they didn't occur to her naturally.

The doorbell rang again.

"What *else* did you do?" Ben's mom asked.

"Nothing!" said Ben, trying to remember whether or not it was true.

I bet it's Nora,

said Ben's dad, walking to the door.

But it wasn't. It was Janet's mom, holding Ben's scooter in one hand and the wing of a great eyeless rainbow-colored sticky-note creature in the other.

In the midst of all the excitement and baseball and pie, Ben had never gone back to check on Janet!

I'm so sorry!

It's okay,

said the sticky-note creature, who didn't seem even sort of mad.

Ben!

I didn't do it!

I mean, I *did* do it, but . . .

I *asked* him to do it,

said the sticky-note creature.

Because I couldn't do it myself.

It's okay. Apparently, this is something she's always wanted to do.

"It could be the last day of my life!" said the sticky-note creature.

"Ugh," said Ben's mom. "Not you, too."

"I'm afraid it's true for all of us, my dear," said Mrs. Ezra, patting Ben's mom on the arm.

"Janet was hoping that one of you might take her picture," said Janet's mom. "My camera isn't working."

"Sure," said Ben's dad, taking out his phone.

They took some photos. And then Janet started removing the sticky notes.

Everyone helped. Slowly Janet began to reappear.

Eventually, her pineapple head popped into view.

Janet's mom gasped.

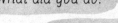

What did you do?

What do you mean?
Janet asked. And then she remembered her haircut.

Oh. Right. That's something *else* I've always wanted to do.

Janet's mom stood there, not crying at first, but then tears started falling like afternoon rain.

"I'm sorry, Mom," said Janet. "I thought you'd like it."

"*I do!* I love it. Your dad was the one who liked your hair long."

"I know," said Janet. "That's why I didn't cut it for forever. But today, I decided it was finally time."

Janet's mom did her best to smile.

I'm really glad you did. And you know what?

You think Dad would like it?

Janet asked hopefully.

Well, maybe. But mostly I know he'd be proud of you for knowing what you wanted to do and then doing it.

The two of them had a hug
that looked big enough for three.

"I know what else I want to do," said Janet when the hug was done.

"What's that?" asked her mom with a slightly worried expression.

"Eat some of that pie."

"That can be arranged," said Ben's mom with a smile.

Ben generously volunteered to have another slice as well, because it would have been rude to make Janet eat pie all by herself.

"Why don't I just cut a piece for everyone?" Mrs. Ezra suggested.

No one had a problem with that.

While Mrs. Ezra served pie and Ben's mom scooped ice cream, Ben excused himself and walked down the hall toward the bathroom, but then he kept going, straight out the back door and into the night.

He had an idea.
A big one.

CHAPTER 34

Ben raced across his backyard, up the oak tree, out onto the big branch, and onto Janet's trampoline.

He opened the black trash can and grabbed the ruined rug, brushing off some leaves and stuffing it into his shirt.

Ben *really* didn't feel like running around the block. He looked over at the fence.

I know I can make it this time, he thought. *It will be the perfect end to my very last day.*

In every Captain A-OK adventure, the Captain would try and fail, again and again, until the final chapter, when he'd attempt the nearly impossible thing for the very last time. And then he'd succeed and save the day against all odds.

Ben wanted to save the day against all odds. He took out his list.

Save the day against all odds

Ben adjusted the rug and tucked in his shirt and ran toward the fence. He timed his jump perfectly. He extended his arms, grabbed the very top of the fence, and almost held on.

Almost.

Ben slid down the fence and landed in an aching heap. He lay there feeling sorry for himself for a full seven seconds, but then he realized: *It is literally impossible to save the day while lying on the ground feeling sorry for myself.*

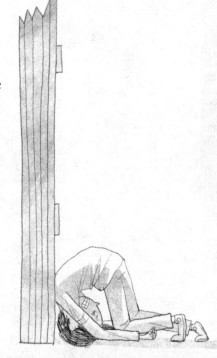

Ben stood up and ran around the block in the direction that didn't involve going past Mr. Hoggenweff's hedge.

When he walked back into the dining room, he was panting and tired and a little bit sweaty. He folded his arms in front of his chest to cover the bulge of the rug.

"Hi, everyone," said Ben, trying to seem normal.

Everyone gave him a look. As far as they knew, he'd been in the bathroom a really long time.

Ben had everyone's attention, so he lifted his shirt and pulled out the rug.

Ta-da! he said, spreading his arms like a magician at the end of a trick.

But no one clapped or smiled or said a word, and Ben instantly understood that he'd said the wrong thing. He wished he'd remembered to prepare for this part of the plan.

"No, Ben!" Janet was furious. She grabbed the rug with one hand and Ben's arm with the other and dragged him into the living room as the adults glanced at each other with wondering eyes.

"What do you think you're doing?" Janet demanded.

Ben said nothing. He was still pretty sure that he'd done the right thing, but he didn't know how to convince Janet.

She had plenty to say on her own.

"You had no right to do that!"

Ben did not defend himself.

"My dad *definitely* wouldn't want my mom to see the rug messed up like that!"

Ben wasn't sure that was true.

"He'd want it to be absolutely *perfect*!"

Janet stopped. She had run out of steam.

Which was good timing. Because

Ben had finally figured out what he

wanted to say.

Someone once told me that a bowl of uncooked spaghetti bits is better than no spaghetti at all.

Why are we talking about spaghetti?

We're not. It's just an example, like the panther and the cupcake. The crunchy spaghetti is the messed-up rug, which, I promise, is better than no rug at all.

Did you *enjoy* the spaghetti, Ben? Because I did not enjoy my pancakes.

It was not delicious, but I'm still glad I tried it.

Aren't you?

Janet thought about that.

Yes, but—

"Someone once told me that you should get a haircut if you want to get a haircut, even if it's not what someone else wants, and even if it ends up looking like a pineapple that got hit by an asteroid."

Janet didn't exactly smile, but her eyes did, just a little, in spite of themselves. Ben thought he was maybe getting somewhere.

"Maybe the point of the fortune isn't to do the things on your list perfectly. After all, a single day is not much time."

It really isn't!

I think the point is that you figure out the things you really want to do and then just do them as well as you possibly can. So at least you know you tried.

Janet sat there for a second, chewing on Ben's words like they were an extremely sticky sandwich.

"I prefer it when I'm the one who says the wise things."

"You said them all first," said Ben. "I'm just reminding you how wise you are."

Ben could see Janet playing Ping-Pong inside her head, part of her wanting to give her mom the rug and part of her wanting to punch Ben in the nose.

You're right, said Janet, taking a deep breath and stretching her back like a panther who has just decided against all odds to give your cupcake back.

When they got back to the dining room, the adults were all sitting there like they were playing chess and it was Janet's turn to make a move.

She handed the rug to her mom.

Dad ... was making this for you. It was supposed to be for your birthday. But if this is the last day of our lives, I'm pretty sure he'd want you to have it now.

Dad made this ...

for me?

Janet's mom made a face like a sunny sky wrestling with a thunderstorm.

"He made part of it," said Janet. "And I made part of it. And Ben made part of it, too."

"I'm the one who made the blue flowers brown," said Ben. "I'm so sorry. But I know we can fix them once we get more yarn."

Janet's mom looked at the brown flowers. "Are these . . . forget-me-nots?" She was looking at the rug the way an owl looks at its nest at the end of a long, cold night.

"Yes!" said Janet. "Your favorite."

"My *very* favorite," said Janet's mom, looking at Janet. She was saying one thing but talking about something else entirely.

"We can fix it tomorrow," said Janet. "I promise. If there *is* a tomorrow, I mean."

"There's *definitely* going to be a tomorrow," said Janet's mom. "But this rug is perfect just the way it is. Just like your haircut. Just like the rest of you. I wouldn't want to change a thing."

There was another great big hug.

No one knew what to say after that, so nobody said anything.

"I don't know about you, but I am getting hungry," said Mrs. Ezra, which helped everyone relax a little.

"Me too!" said Ben, as he stared lovingly at his piece of pie.

For a minute or two, the only sound was the clinking of forks against plates.

But then Janet sighed and smiled and said, "This is really, *really* good."

Ben wanted to agree, but he was feeling somewhat queasy. For the first time in his life, he wondered if maybe he'd had too much dessert for one day.

Well? said Mrs. Ezra, looking at Janet.

Well . . . *what?* said Janet, who had never been this close to Mrs. Ezra and didn't look entirely happy about it.

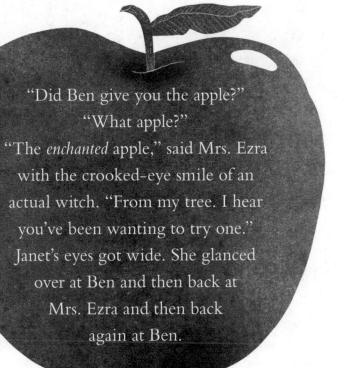

"Did Ben give you the apple?"

"What apple?"

"The *enchanted* apple," said Mrs. Ezra with the crooked-eye smile of an actual witch. "From my tree. I hear you've been wanting to try one."

Janet's eyes got wide. She glanced over at Ben and then back at Mrs. Ezra and then back again at Ben.

"Don't worry," said Mrs. Ezra, patting Janet on her hand. "I have enough trolls for the time being."

"*Trolls?*" asked Janet's mom.

"Trolls," said Mrs. Ezra. "They help me fold the laundry."

Janet's mom smiled politely and ate her pie. She had heard the stories about Mrs. Ezra, too.

Ben raced into the kitchen to get Janet's apple but couldn't find it anywhere.

Did anyone see an apple in here?

he shouted.

Was it deepest red and perfectly shaped and extremely delicious?

his dad asked.

That sounds just like it,

said Ben, his heart sinking like a rock in a pond.

I'm sorry, Ben, said his dad, who really did look sorry.

I was hungry after my long drive. Next time if you don't want me to eat something that belongs to you, just write a note. I find that works pretty well.

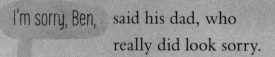

"Great idea,"
said Ben, glancing over at his
mom, who was making her *You're not
going to get any sympathy from me, mister* face.
"Don't worry," said Mrs. Ezra. "I know where
you can find another one. Or another one
hundred. Why don't you two come over tomorrow
and help me pick a few?"
"Sure!" said Ben, suddenly remembering that apples
grow on trees and wishing that apple pies did, too.
"Okay," said Janet, who seemed worried that even
if today wasn't her last day as a living person,
tomorrow could be her first day as a laundry-
folding troll.

CHAPTER 35

After that, Janet and her mom and Mrs. Ezra all went home, and Ben's mom went upstairs to get ready, and Aunt Nora showed up and apologized to Ben's dad for being so late.

But somehow, she was also right on time. That's the kind of weird and wonderful day it had been. Ben looked at the clock. The day was almost over.

He looked at his list and felt good. He'd accomplished so much. But not quite everything.

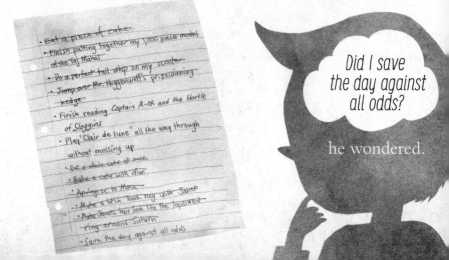

- Eat a piece of cake
- Finish putting together my 1,000 piece model of the Taj Mahal
- Do a perfect tail whip on my scooter
- Jump over Mr. Heggenwell's prizewinning hedge
- Finish reading Captain A-ok and the Hortle of Sloggins
- Play "Clair de lune" all the way through without messing up
- Eat a whole cake at once
- Bake a cake with Milan
- Apologize to Mom
- Make a latch hook rug with Janet
- Make Janet's hair look like the lopsided ring around Saturn
- Save the day against all odds

Did I save the day against all odds?

he wondered.

Ben thought he probably had.

But he still needed to play "Clair de lune" without messing up. And he still needed to finish reading *Captain A-OK and the Hortle of Sloggins*.

He tried playing "Clair de lune" but mangled it so badly that Dumbles howled and hid under the sofa. Ben suddenly realized how tired he was.

It wasn't really time yet, but Ben got in bed anyway. He had just started chapter six of *Captain A-OK and the Hortle of Sloggins* for the second time that day when his mom and dad appeared in his doorway.

Ben's dad was carrying a shoebox that Ben assumed contained a piece of cake. He smiled down at Ben without a hint of suspicion.

"We wondered if you'd like to come to dinner with us," his mom said.

"But isn't this your nine years, three months, and seventeen days anniversary?"

"Yes, but you're the best thing about the first nine years, three months, and seventeen days of being married," said his dad.

"If this is the last dinner of our lives, we both want to eat it with you," said his mom.

Ben was relieved to hear it. He felt like he'd been nothing but trouble all day.

"I'd like to," said Ben, "but if this is the last night of my life, I'd mostly like to get some sleep."

The three of them had a great big pretzel of a hug. It was something they hadn't done in a long time.

And then his parents left, and it was just Ben and his list and *Captain A-OK*. Ben returned to chapter six.

He didn't make it to chapter seven.

CHAPTER 36

Ben woke up at 12:01 a.m. Because his alarm was still set to 12:01 a.m.

He had two thoughts. The first thought was *I guess yesterday* wasn't *my last day.* And the second was *I'm really looking forward to* this *day.*

Ben glanced over at the table by his bed. There was a fortune cookie with a note taped to it. Ben could tell from the handwriting that it was from his dad.

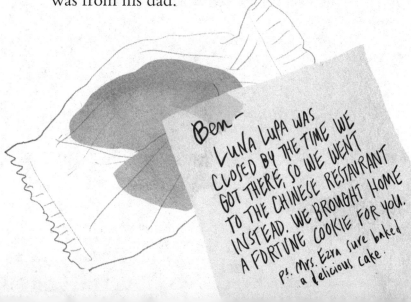

Ben —
LUNA LUPA WAS CLOSED BY THE TIME WE GOT THERE, SO WE WENT TO THE CHINESE RESTAURANT INSTEAD. WE BROUGHT HOME A FORTUNE COOKIE FOR YOU.
P.S. Mrs. Ezra sure baked a delicious cake.

At first, Ben was relieved that his dad didn't seem mad about the replacement cake. But then he started wondering where his mom had hidden the *rest* of the replacement cake.

Finally, he opened the cookie and read the fortune.

> *The search for happiness begins with a single step.*

That's really smart advice, thought Ben as he reset his alarm. *At exactly 7:03 a.m., I am going to search for happiness by stepping out of bed and finding the rest of Mrs. Ezra's cake.*

By the time Ben got to the word "cake," he was already asleep and dreaming.

Cake dreams were Ben's favorite kind.

Hi, I'm Matthew. I wrote this book.

I'm Robbi. I drew the pictures.

ABOUT THE AUTHOR AND ILLUSTRATOR

Matthew: They are extremely nice pictures. *Extremely.*

Robbi: Now I am suspicious. Are you just complimenting my drawings so that I'll say nice things about your words?

M: *Absolutely.* Flatter me, please.

Hm. Okay. Let's see. *Hey, Matthew. Your writing. It's so good.*

That was an excellent first draft, but could you try again, this time with more exciting adjectives?

Sorry, but that's *your* job, word person. If you tell me an adjective, I will gladly illustrate it for you. Or you could tell these nice people why you wrote this book.

M: That's easy. I wrote this book because I'm extremely fond of cake.

R: *Please don't lie to our readers!* You don't like cake at all. You always complain that cake is too dry.

M: Yes, and also so crumbly! But here's the truth: I have *no idea* why I wrote this book. My creative process is a murky swamp where I thrash about frantically while looking for something to hold on to. I think I wrote this book because Ben grabbed me by the arm and yanked me out of the muck and told me it was the last day of his life, which sounded interesting. So I followed him around and wrote down everything he did, said, and ate.

I think we should have stuck with the cake theory.

M: Why did you illustrate this book?

R: Wasn't there something in our wedding vows like, *I promise to love and support you, blah, blah, blah*? I consider illustrating your books part of the *blah, blah*. I'd do it for anyone I married. I thank my stars every day that I didn't marry Stephen King.

R: I'd be happy to—*if* I weren't so busy illustrating your books. You write a lot of books, mister. They might not be as creepy as Stephen King's, but there are just as many! Would you please start writing fewer books? Illustrating books is the worst!

M: Now *you're* lying to our readers! Admit it, you *enjoyed* illustrating this book!

M: Are you saying that this book about Ben is actually a story about . . . you?

R: Sort of. If you insist. But also, I'm a lot like Janet. She's tough and strong and smart and extremely sure of herself.

M: So . . . you're Ben *and* Janet?

R: Pretty much. But now that I think of it, I'm also a lot like Ben's mom, who tells it like it is, doesn't put up with nonsense, and drives a blue car.

Do *I* get to be in this book?

Of course. You're Ben's dad. He's super nice, loves his kid, and is willing to drive a long way to buy his wife some ice cream. What I'm trying to say is that you're great. Terrible haircut and all.

For the record, I'm not driving six hours to get you ice cream. I have several more books to write.

I suddenly regret all those compliments.

M: What else should we tell these folks? Should we let them know that we're married?

R: I think they got that from the mention of wedding vows. Our readers are bright, Matthew.

M: But should we tell them that we have four kids?

R: I think they probably got that from the bags beneath my eyes and your awful dad jokes. Our readers are not just bright, but extremely observant.

M: Should we tell them that *The Cookie of Doom* is just the first book in an ongoing series about Ben and his cookie-based adventures?

R: Are you trying to sell our books to these nice people? That's *shameless*!

M: Sorry, but I think that was also part of the *blah, blah, blah.*

Oh, right! Buy more books, folks! Books are virtuous! BOOKS! BOOKS! BOOKS!

M: That's more like it. Now, would you please fix the faucet?

R: Only if you drive six hours to buy me some ice cream. *Do we have a deal?*

To get on our mailing list, write us a note, or ask us to speak at your school, library, or conference, visit us at

robbiandmatthew.com

Thank you for reading our book!

Blah, blah, blah!

FORTUNE COOKIE FACTS

Chances are, you've eaten a fortune cookie—that small and crunchy folded treat made from flour, sugar, butter, egg whites, and vanilla that is mixed together in a vat, then squirted onto heated trays on a conveyor belt before being compressed and cooked . . .

and then fed into a special machine that fills each one with wisdom and molds them into shape.

Chances are, you got your fortune cookie at a Chinese restaurant. But fortune cookies were actually first made in nineteenth-century Japan, in the city of Kyoto. They were slightly larger than today's cookies, and their batter was darker and flavored with miso (a paste made from fermented soybeans) and sesame seeds instead of vanilla. But they did contain a fortune.

The first fortune cookies in the United States were served at the Japanese Tea Garden in San Francisco at the turn of the twentieth century by a man named Makoto Hagiwara.

Unless you believe the claim of David Jung of the Hong Kong Noodle Company, who insisted that he invented the fortune cookie in Los Angeles in 1918.

Because the origin of cookies is such serious business, San Francisco and Los Angeles had a great big argument and eventually had no choice but to take legal action.

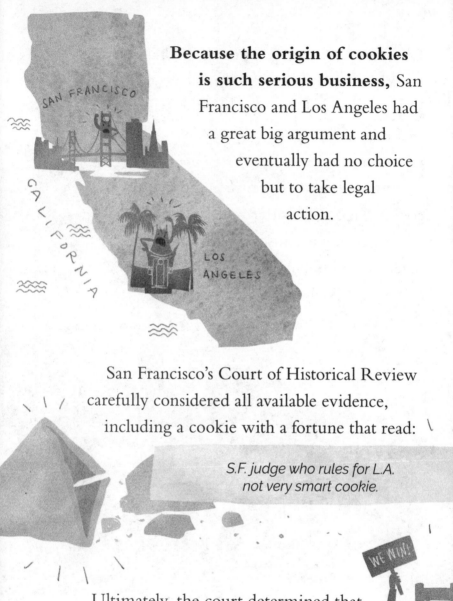

San Francisco's Court of Historical Review carefully considered all available evidence, including a cookie with a fortune that read:

*S.F. judge who rules for L.A.
not very smart cookie.*

Ultimately, the court determined that Hagiwara was the first to serve the cookie in America and that San Francisco was free to claim bragging rights.

Los Angeles is still not happy about it.

ABOUT 3 BILLION FORTUNE COOKIES ARE MADE EACH YEAR

They are served in Chinese restaurants around the world but aren't particularly popular in China itself. In fact, most of them are eaten in America.

Which is to say, although they may have originated in nineteenth-century Japan and are most often found at Chinese restaurants, fortune cookies are a distinctly American phenomenon.

Just like Ben.

273

Join Ben on his latest adventure!

CHAPTER 1

Ben Yokoyama had a pretty good life.

He lived with his mom and his dad in a house that had three ceiling fans, a garbage disposal, and a roof that didn't leak when it rained.

He had a dog named Dumbles, who would sometimes fetch a tennis ball and often gave cuddles and licks.

His best friend, Janet, lived in the house just behind his. She had a trampoline, a comfortable blue chair, and a pantry that usually contained marshmallows.

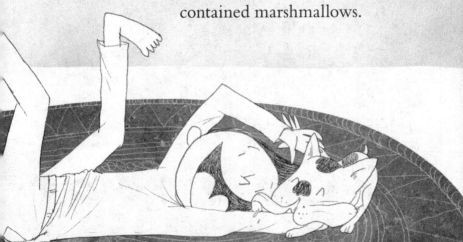

Ben had nothing to complain about, so he usually didn't complain. But some days, he had to. Because some days, his mom burned the pancakes.

Sorry, Ben! said Ben's mom, setting a plateful of scorched, food-like slabs on the table.

They're a little bit crispy.

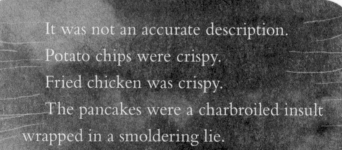

It was not an accurate description.
Potato chips were crispy.
Fried chicken was crispy.
The pancakes were a charbroiled insult wrapped in a smoldering lie.
"That's okay," said Ben the way someone might say,
What's that awful smell?
when a wet goat walks into the room.

WHAT...?

"Look," said Ben's mom, bending down and offering Dumbles a pancake. "Dumby likes them."

Dumbles took one sniff of the not-a-pancake and fled into the living room.

"Good boy," said Ben's dad, who had once read in a magazine that it was unhealthy for dogs to eat human food.

"How about you, Ken?" asked Ben's mom.

"You know . . . I just remembered that we're having a *special* breakfast at work today. Martha is bringing muffins."

"But you don't *like* muffins."

"Maybe today is the day I finally will! I always tell *Ben* to keep an open mind."

Ben's dad was a terrible liar. Saying anything but the truth made him sweaty and cross-eyed.

Ben's mom made a face that said, *I wish you could see how sweaty and cross-eyed you look.*

"I could have . . . maybe just . . . *one* of these pancakes without ruining my appetite," Ben's dad offered.

"It would be my *pleasure* to serve you one," said Ben's mom, placing three singed wafers of unparalleled sadness on his plate.

Usually Ben's dad made breakfast. And dinner. And lunch on the weekends. Because he was just so much better at cooking. For her part, Ben's mom changed the oil in the car and used the chainsaw to lop off suspicious-looking tree limbs.

But Ben's mom was trying to learn how to cook, so they had started *Monday Meals with Mom!* The idea had seemed so great before the actual cooking began.

Ben had even made a sign. He now regretted the exclamation point.

Ben's dad picked up his fork and knife and cut a bite so small it wouldn't have made a hungry hamster happy.

"I guess the rest of these *delicious* pancakes are all for you, Ben," said his mom, sliding six discs of blackened apocalypse onto his plate.

Ben panicked. It was a family rule that you had to eat *everything* on your plate, whether you liked it or not.

MONDAY
MEALS
→ WITH MOM!

He reached down into the center of his misery and came back with an idea.

> What about *you*, Mom? It wouldn't be right to take all these pancakes for myself. I insist you have at least four.

"I'm on a diet," she snapped.

"You *are*?" This was news to Ben. He had seen her eat a full rack of ribs the night before.

"But *why*?" asked Ben's dad.

HEALTH, said Ben's mom with the frosty resolve of a snowcapped Himalaya.

Ben's mom was an *excellent* liar. Ben looked at his dad. His dad looked at Ben. They both looked at Ben's mom wide-eyed, like someone who has just read the first chapter of a thrilling mystery and is desperate to know how it ends.

"Nora is on a special diet where she eats nothing but ground beef and bananas," Ben's mom continued. "I've decided to try it."

Nora was Ben's aunt. Ben liked Nora a lot, but Ben's mom usually rolled her eyes at the things Nora did, said, wore, and ate. Never in her whole life had Ben's mom done something just because Aunt Nora did.

"Well, why don't you grab a banana and join us?" Ben's dad suggested, patting the place mat beside him.

But the fruit bowl was empty.

I ate my bananas before you guys got up,

said Ben's mom with a look that was ever-so-slightly cross-eyed.

That's strange. I didn't see any peels when I emptied the trash can earlier.

I also ate the peels,

said Ben's mom, looking somewhat sweaty now, too.

Ben was starting to wonder if maybe his mom wasn't such an excellent liar after all.

"That's an *interesting* diet," said Ben. It seemed impossible that eating banana peels was a good idea in any universe. He couldn't wait to ask Nora if it was true.

"Oh yes. It's quite something," said Ben's mom. "Now, please, my men. Enjoy your meal."

But asking Ben to enjoy the pancakes was like asking a snowman to enjoy a cup of hot chocolate. He searched the distant corners of his mind for a way to get around the problem.

He could dump his pancakes on the floor and hope that no one noticed. He could run out the door and never come back. Or . . .

Ben had a better idea. A simpler one. He looked down at his watch and very much liked what he saw.

Oh *shucks*, would you look at the time? I really *must* be going,

he said, standing up and carrying his plate across the room in one fluid motion.

If I don't leave now, I might be late to meet Janet at the corner. And you know how I feel about being late.

We sure do,

said Ben's dad, like one wobbling bowling pin says to another.

Don't we, Linda?

I am familiar with your legendary punctuality,

said Ben's mom, like the ball as it races down the lane.

I'm *just so sorry* that I don't have time to finish my *delicious* pancakes,

said Ben as he placed his untouched plateful of crunchy despair in the sink. Ben was a better liar than his dad but not nearly as good as his mom.

He grabbed his coat and his backpack and was halfway out the door when his dad said, "Wait!"

Ben thought about making a break for it. One more step and he'd be free of the horrible pancakes forever.

"Your jersey!" his dad continued.

Suddenly Ben remembered. He had asked his dad to wash his jersey so he could wear it to school.

"Thanks," said Ben, taking the jersey. He was about to put it on when he noticed something.

What ... *happened?*

It wasn't an actual question, because the answer didn't really matter. What mattered was the endless mess of greasy blotches all over his jersey.

Oh, Ken,

said Ben's mom.

Well, shucks, said Ben's dad without further explanation. Because no further explanation was needed. Ben and his mom knew this story pretty well.

Sometimes, or maybe even often, Ben's dad left tubes of lip balm in the pocket of his pants when he put them in the laundry, which meant they melted in the dryer and left great greasy blotches all over the clothes.

Ben was only halfway mad when his socks got greasy or his *Ski Minnesota!* sweatshirt got blotchy, but his jersey was *different*.

It was the jersey of first baseman Pete (The Big) Bubango of the Honeycutt Melons. *The Big Bubango had signed it himself!*

"I'm so sorry," said Ben's dad.

Ben was speechless. "Sorry" was for when you accidentally bumped into someone in the cafeteria and made them spill their milk a little.

This was a moment for shouting forbidden words as sky-splitting lightning sets nearby trees on fire.

His once-in-a-lifetime jersey was ruined.

"Maybe I can get it out with that special spray I bought for grass stains," said Ben's mom with her *All is not lost* face.

"I thought that spray didn't really work," said Ben's dad with his *Of course I hope it works, but I don't want to get Ben's hopes up* face.

"It didn't work for jeans. But maybe it *will* work for Ben's jersey," said Ben's mom with her *Hope is not a strategy* face.

Ben looked at his watch. If he didn't leave right away, he actually *would* be late.

Ben's mom squirted and scrubbed and examined and sighed and squirted and scrubbed and scrubbed and scowled and, eventually, rinsed.

Ben's heart hoped for a clean jersey the way someone hopes for sunshine on the morning of his outdoor birthday party.

"Hmm," said Ben's mom, handing the jersey to Ben. It wasn't an encouraging sound. "I think it looks *much* better now."

Ben did not agree. The jersey was just as greasy as it had been before. But now it was also damp. Ben scowled like someone whose birthday party has just been canceled due to hail.

"It will look better when it dries," said Ben's mom unconvincingly.

Ben took off his shirt and put on his jersey instead. He felt hungry, greasy, wet, and cold.

Some days just don't start out the way you want them to,

said his dad, putting his arms around Ben and pulling him in for a hug.

But it doesn't mean they have to *end* that way. You never know what today might bring.

Usually his dad's pep talks did the trick, but today Ben didn't *want* to be cheered up.

He flew out the door and raced to the corner with the yellow bush, determined to get there on time.

While Ben sprinted his way along the sidewalk, he thought about the things he wanted.

Pancakes that weren't burnt.

A clean, dry jersey.

And to get to the corner on time.

It didn't seem like a lot to ask.

Ben looked at his watch and ran faster. He got there with seventeen seconds to spare.

Then he waited.

And waited.

Because Janet was late.

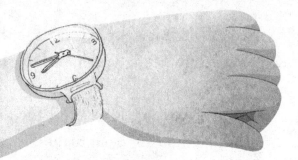

CHAPTER 2

Janet was often late.

Most mornings, Ben didn't mind. Because waiting meant time to make up limericks or search for four-leaf clovers. But today he was already halfway mad, and the waiting made him madder.

Two minutes passed. Then seven. Then thirteen.

Eventually, Janet showed up.

"Good morning," she said with a smile.

Ben looked away. Janet's smile had a way of warming him up, and he wanted to stay chilly for a while. He started marching down the sidewalk toward the school.

Janet scurried to keep up.

What's your deal? she asked, trying to catch her breath.

You're late.

Janet looked at her watch and shrugged.

I'm exactly as late as I was on Friday.

Exactly, said Ben. As far as he was
concerned, Janet was
making his point for him.

Friday you didn't stomp away
the second I showed up.

That was true. But on Friday Ben hadn't been
hungry and grease-stained and wet. He knew
that Janet was only partly responsible for his
bad mood. But he wanted her to take the whole
blame.

Ben marched on in a hurried huff.

"Sheesh," said Janet with breathless exasperation. "Would you hold on a second? I have something for you."

That got Ben's attention. Getting something was better than being mad. He took a deep breath and told the angry part of him to take a five-minute time-out.

"What is it?"

"Mom and I went to the Chinese restaurant last night. I saved my fortune cookie for you."

"Oh," said Ben, trying to seem less excited than he actually was.

Thanks.

Janet smiled. She knew that Ben's two soft spots were delicious desserts and wise words. Fortune cookies had *both*.

Ben cracked open the cookie and read the fortune.

Practice makes perfect.

The wisdom hit Ben like the sunrise hits the early-morning shadows. Suddenly everything was perfectly clear!

It *wasn't* that his parents were hopeless.

Janet *wasn't* a lost cause.

It was *entirely possible* that all three of them might *eventually* be perfect.

They just had some practicing to do.

THE COOKIE CHRONICLES

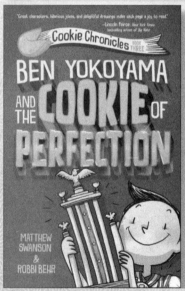

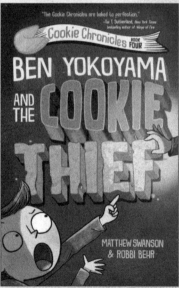

DON'T MISS A SINGLE BITE!